THE INSULTING OFFER W9-ABN-962

"You will not wish to wed a penniless orphan, Mr. Thorne," Fenella forced herself to say. "Do not feel you have to offer for me."

"I *have* offered," Robert said, and added, "It is much the best thing for you to do."

Had he swooped her up in his arms, he might have prevailed. But he did not. This was not the gallant who had won her heart. She did not recognize the man standing before her.

"The best thing for me?" she echoed. "But not for you, is that your meaning?"

Robert turned ashen. "You think I offered from *duty*?" His eyes dark in his pale face, he turned and walked out of Fenella's life . . .

. . . until they met again.

About the Author

Vanessa Gray grew up in Oak Park, Illinois, and graduated from the University of Chicago. She currently lives in the farm country of northeastern Indiana, where she pursues her interest in the history of Georgian England and the Middle Ages. She is the author of a number of bestselling Regencies available in Signet editions.

The Lady's Revenge

Vanessa Gray

A SIGNET BOOK

NEW AMERICAN LIBRARY

A DIVISION OF PENGUIN BOOKS USA INC.

NAL BOOKS ARE AVAILABLE AT QUANTITY DISCOUNTS WHEN USED TO
PROMOTE PRODUCTS OR SERVICES. FOR INFORMATION PLEASE WRITE TO
PREMIUM MARKETING DIVISION. NEW AMERICAN LIBRARY.
1633 BROADWAY. NEW YORK. NEW YORK 10019.

 SIGNET TRADEMARK REG. U.S.PAT. OFF. AND FOREIGN COUNTRIES
REGISTERED TRADEMARK—MARCA REGISTRADA
HECHO EN DRESDEN. TN. U.S.A.

SIGNET, SIGNET CLASSIC, MENTOR, ONYX, PLUME, MERIDIAN
and NAL BOOKS are published by New American Library,
a division of Penguin Books USA Inc., 1633 Broadway,
New York, New York 10019

First Printing, September, 1989

1   2   3   4   5   6   7   8   9

PRINTED IN THE UNITED STATES OF AMERICA

1

The Wednesday-evening gathering in Almack's Assembly Rooms in King Street paid little heed to the weather outside. No matter that a stifling drought had gripped the dusty land all through March and now into April. The social whirl continued without cessation.

This day, late afternoon had provided a cloud bank, somewhat bigger than a man's hand, rising in the west, and by the time carriages began to arrive before the door of the Assembly Rooms, lightning was flashing in the skies over west London, and thunder muttered in the distance like cannon.

More than one formerly military gentleman, politely helping his lady down from the carriage, restrained with difficulty a long-ingrained impulse to dive for shelter under the nearest vehicle. Peacetime was not supposed to sound so very much like battle.

When Gerald Lanceford handed down his betrothed, Fenella Standish, from her father's carriage, he had no such impulse. He had not gone to the Peninsula to fight under Wellington. Nor had he stirred from London at any time during the past years, save to journey to Oakhurst, Sir Giles Standish's country seat in Dorset, where he had paid languid court to Sir Giles's only child.

Gerald knew that Fenella had no significant fortune, and it was even rumored that, since his own lack of fortune and character was becoming increasingly well-known, the lady might be his only chance of marriage. Besides, if her father would deed over two farms that Gerald held in his mind's eye, she would come as well-dowered as he had any hopes of. Gerald thought that the formal announcement of the engagement would bring Sir Giles up to the mark, but so far no mention of a marriage settlement had been forthcoming.

But at least, since the betrothal had been announced, no other swain would develop a claim on Gerald's two farms!

As usual on Wednesday evenings during the Season, linkboys and other hangers-on lingered in King Street in the shadows surrounding the brightly lit entrance, avid to see the bright, glittering ladies and gentlemen of society. Fenella was one of their favorites, not only because of her lovely gowns and furs, but also because of the brilliance of her smile in response to the cheers of the crowds in the shadows.

While it was considered most improper to recognize even the existence of those men and women who haunted the out-skirts of any grand occasion, Fenella always sent a shining glance into the shadows, and smiled.

Gerald tugged at her sleeve. "Don't encourage them!" he ordered. "You never know what they will do."

"I cannot think a mere smile will incite Londoners to riot," she said gently. Tonight was not the time to become annoyed with Gerald. He had been out of town for a fortnight, and as a betrothed lady, her social events had been limited. Now he was back, and she intended to dance the night away under the watchful eyes of the Countess of Jersey, Princess Esterhazy, and the five other patronesses.

Already the violins were calling for the first dance. Gerald looked down at his fiancée, barely down, for he was only an inch or two taller than Fenella. She was so pretty, he thought, congratulating himself on his luck. Not always were a pleasant countenance and an amiable disposition coupled with an adequate income, and while it was the latter that Gerald's creditors demanded, he would not deny the former qualities would make life more pleasant.

If only Sir Giles would come to terms on the marriage settlement!

Fenella stopped to speak to those of the patronesses who

were receiving. Lady Cowper pulled her aside. Casting a glance at Gerald, Lady Cowper said gaily, "You know, Mr. Lanceford, you must not keep Fenella all to yourself. We have known her quite a bit longer than you have, sir! Fenella, I want a word with you." She turned her back on him then, to indicate that his presence was not required. Fenella cast a rueful glance at Gerald, intending to indicate by a faint shrug of her bare shoulders that she was helpless to resist. But Gerald had already turned away.

"My dear," said Lady Cowper, "you have been secluding yourself far too much. I did not see you at Devonshire House last evening."

"Gerald was out of London," Fenella explained.

"But you should not give up all your friends. I should have sent someone for you, rather than let you languish alone."

Fenella smiled. Her generous mouth turned up at the corners in a beguiling way, and Lady Cowper sighed inwardly. Such a waste!

"My dear," she said, "there is someone I want you to meet. He's just back from a brilliant career on dear Arthur's staff."

"Another general?" quizzed Fenella. "I have had my fill of military men. They wish to turn the world into a parade ground."

"Not this one, my dear. I do not even know his rank, for he refuses to use it, and I have been told he will not answer to it. I saw him a moment ago. You cannot miss him. He is head and shoulders taller than any man here tonight."

Fenella said, "Perhaps later, Lady Cowper. Just now I must find Gerald."

Lady Cowper thought: Let him remain lost—but she said only, "You really must meet this young man."

Fenella was not deceived. She knew that Lady Cowper, as well as certain other ladies, who had for the most part been friends of her late mother's—deceased so long ago Fenella could barely remember her—did not approve of her coming marriage to Gerald, and she knew as well that the returned soldier was another of the ploys to lure her away from him.

But she was betrothed to Gerald, the announcement had been in the *Gazette,* and there was no turning back.

The evening went swiftly for Fenella, sped by lilting music and the figures of the dance, and it was nearly suppertime. The usual fare at the Assembly Rooms consisted of small sandwiches, some inferior punch, and cakes which atoned for their staleness by their minuscule size. Fenella did not hurry to the supper rooms.

A heavy drumming on the roof of the building told her that the storm had broken. The moist scent of London air that stole in through the outer doors when they were opened for a moment would revive even the most jaded.

Gerald had disappeared once again. She moved to the door of the supper rooms and waited. He would look for her here, and they would go in to supper together. It occurred to her that perhaps a fiancé might be expected to remain within sight of his lady, but Gerald had a propensity to do as he pleased.

She glanced out over the crowd, looking for Gerald. He was not tall enough for her to see easily, and her attention was snared by individual faces. She was acquainted with most of them, of course. Suddenly one particular figure caught her eye—a man, a gentleman of course, or he would not have been admitted, of unusual height. Gerald would have come up scarcely to his shoulder.

He was a stranger to Fenella. She knew she would have remembered had she seen him before. His hair was dark, and he was dressed well but soberly. From this distance she could not be sure of his eyes, but she had a feeling they would be blue, blue as the North Sea. Perhaps it was the intensity of her gaze that reached him. At any rate, he turned his head and looked directly at her.

She felt a tightness in her chest. The sensation lasted only a couple of seconds, and she could breathe again.

"Have you been waiting long?" came Gerald's cool voice in her ear. "My apologies."

She wrenched her gaze from the stranger and looked at Gerald. "Who is that man?" she asked, but when she tried to point him out to Gerald, the stranger had vanished.

"Never mind, he's gone. Let's go in to supper. I'm famished."

But when at last she was faced with little strips of bread and butter, and weak raspberry punch, she ate very little. That strange sensation she had felt just before Gerald had come for her was a warning, she told herself, a harbinger of a digestive upset. It could be nothing else, she decided, and therefore it seemed advisable to eat lightly.

At last Gerald was ready to leave. He had sent for the coach, and Fenella, her cloak around her shoulders, waited for him inside the doors. How stuffy it was!

On an impulse, she spoke to the attendant. "Pray open the door. I vow I am nearly stifled by the close air within."

"But, miss, it's *raining* out there!"

"So it is," said Fenella, unmoved, "but it is only water, after all."

She smiled at him, and, as had many another male, he leaped to do her bidding. She stepped quickly out onto the pavement. Carriages were lined up along King Street as far as St. James's Street. She could hear above the rain and the thunder the sound of restless stamping of hooves and soothing voices of grooms all along the line of vehicles.

The storm was receding although there lingered an occasional flash of lightning, and roll of thunder. The air was still oppressive. She glanced apprehensively toward the west, where another storm seemed to be rushing toward London.

Always, after a long period of heat and stuffiness, when the storms came, they came in force. The fresh air was marvelously refreshing, and she welcomed it. But soon a tiny frown appeared between her brows and she was conscious of a desire to tap her foot in irritation. Where was Gerald? She had a very good idea of what he was doing, since when he had returned to her after other absences this evening she had sniffed the aroma of strong liquor.

She was aware of the doorman keeping an unobtrusive eye on her, but she was not in the least alarmed. The town air, even rain-washed as it was, was no more unhealthy than the air of Dorset.

She was content to watch the new storm approaching, seeing the lightning illuminate west London. Suddenly she was aroused from her abstracted air. The second storm was almost overhead now. The rain began to pour in sheets, spattering her cloak even though she huddled against the wall of the building.

All at once everything changed.

The scene was lit by continuing flashes of lightning. In the intervals the torches of the linkboys and the fixed torches at the entrance doors were too feeble to illuminate any space beyond them. Besides, the lightning blinded her until the next flash stabbed the sky.

The incessant lightning turned the very air the color of lavender. At almost the same instant, the thunder boomed. And the horses had had enough.

Fenella had a very confused impression of what happened next. She saw the lightning, of course, and smelled the peculiar acrid odor that usually followed a direct hit somewhere nearby. The horses suddenly took panic, leaping and rearing in their fright, splitting the air with their frenzied high-pitched whinnies, as though facing enemy cannon.

There was the rending sound of shafts being smashed under the horses' plunging, the heavy sound of hooves coming down on the pavement from a height. And the sound of galloping hooves rushing toward her on the pavement.

It all happened so fast!

For a moment she did not see her own danger. When she did, her feet froze to the pavement and she could not move.

The crowd moaned as one, a sound to raise the hackles. Suddenly a man emerged from the door, took in the situation at a glance, and shoved her without ceremony against the wall, thrusting his own body between her and the rampaging horse.

She gasped with the shock of speeding events. The words "how dare you" formed for an instant on her lips and vanished, to be followed by a fervent "Thank God!", but since her face was pressed into a muscular shoulder, she could not vent her feelings.

She could not move away either, for the man held her tightly in a grip like iron, long after the sound of hoofbeats and shouting had receded toward Duke Street. Her wits flew, to make sense of this. Her rescuer was obviously a gentleman, for the scent of shaving soap was fresh. Not Gerald, for this man was much taller. As tall, even as the stranger she had noticed across the room.

She was aware of a kind of convulsion in the hard chest into which she realized, with shame, she was burrowing her face. The man was laughing!

She gasped and tried to pull herself away. She could not see his features, for the dark, but she heard his words, heard them very distinctly, in a low voice that rumbled in his chest, against her ear. "Don't worry. I shan't seduce you here on the doorstep of Almack's!" he assured her.

She looked up into his face. The hood of her wrap fell back, and torchlight flickered over her face. He took note of the level gaze fixed on him, the eyebrows sweeping upward at the outer edge like gulls' wings, the straight nose. In an altered tone he said thoughtfully, "Perhaps another time."

By the time she had regained the power of speech, he had released her and was striding away down the pavement. No need of a carriage, apparently, so he must live nearby.

The impertinent wretch! What did she care where he lived?

Seduce her! She sputtered in indignation. She realized that she had not the slightest idea who he was, save that his height declared him to be Lady Cowper's protégé, almost certainly the man she had seen across the room for that arresting moment. It had been dark, still was dark, and now that she looked again, he was out of sight. And she had never thanked him!

Gerald was pulling at her cloak. "What was all that about, Fenella?"

Looking around her, she saw a carriage pulled out of the way, bereft of one wheel, and the remaining one of a pair of horses still struggling, but with lessening panic now that the storm had moved on.

Even yet feeling the stranger's protective arms about her, and only now beginning to understand fully the extreme danger she had escaped, she said, "Nothing at all, Gerald." She knew he was eyeing her suspiciously, and she really could not blame him. What he had seen when he emerged from Almack's, his vision possibly blurred by recent imbib-

ing, must have given pause to the most lenient fiancé: his
lady all but smothered in the grasp of a large man who suddenly stood her up on her feet and swiftly vanished down
the street.

But lest Fenella begin to question his own whereabouts
in a time of her need—and Gerald had garnered sufficient
details when he emerged from the building to know that her
peril had been real and grave—he decided to let the matter
drop. Fenella was his, and she would never cry off. She was
too honest to jilt him. And he would make sure they were
wed as soon as Sir Giles could be brought up to the mark
on the settlement. The pair of good farms Gerald coveted
was, if he played his cards right, only a start.

Tomorrow he would press his claim with the old man.

But when he brought Fenella into the foyer of the house
Sir Giles had hired for the Season, he met Sir Giles's cold
eyes and his plans changed abruptly. Sir Giles had not approved of Gerald at the start, but had given in, thinking to
please his daughter. But, Gerald guessed correctly, it would
take little for Sir Giles to alter his mind.

Gerald dared not chance his fate.

2

Not until the following Wednesday did Fenella again meet her handsome rescuer.

That is not to say she did not think of him during that sennight, for she did. She scanned every crowd at every party she went to, but the tall figure she hoped to see did not appear. If he had been at Almack's, then he was sure to be welcome in all the great houses of London, as she herself was. At last she decided that either his tastes did not run to friendly intercourse with those of his own quality, or she had imagined the entire incident.

But she had not fancied those strong arms around her, nor that amused voice promising not to seduce her—at least not that night!

The man was not a figment of her imagination. When she entered Almack's, escorted this time, since Gerald had pleaded another engagement, by Lady Montague, an old acquaintance of her father's, the stranger stood beyond the patronesses, scanning each new arrival as though searching for someone.

Lady Cowper pulled Fenella away from Lady Montague and spoke earnestly to her. "You recall last week I wanted to present someone to you? I have the gentleman at hand. Now, my dear, I wish to hear no protestations, for this is the man you should wed. Believe me, I know what I say."

"Lady Cowper," said Fenella faintly, "you forget Gerald Lanceford."

"Assuredly I do not forget him. But he will not trouble

you this evening, for I have certain information he is playing at Crockford's tonight!''

She made a slight gesture, and at once the tall stranger was beside her.

"Miss Standish," said Lady Cowper, "allow me to present Mr. Thorne. I believe he dances well, at least his mother tells me so, for you must know she and I have been friends for a long time. Now, Robert, you are properly introduced.''

Fenella was understandably shy. Having this tall, broad-shouldered gentleman, her rescuer, stroll amiably through her dreams was one thing, but having him presented so abruptly, with the added recommendation that she wed him, was outside of enough. How much had he heard?

Too much, as it happened. "Lady Cowper is certainly outspoken," said Mr. Thorne. "I envy her, in a way.''

"How is that?''

''I have never been so sure of my own opinions as to know what is best for all my acquaintances.'' Then, thoughtfully, he added, ''However, she is most often right, you know.''

Fenella found the room overly warm, and brought her tiny fan into play.

''Shall we find a place to sit?'' He touched her arm and guided her to a settee on the far side of the room, away from the gaze of new arrivals, yet decorously situated. ''Let us not tease ourselves over Lady Cowper's judgments. I must tell you that I have watched for you at every affair I attended this week.''

She looked up. You too? she thought, but did not say. The expression in his dark blue eyes was unsettling, and she hardly knew how to answer him. Bemused, she was aware only of the clean aura that surrounded him, as though he had been dipped in soap. Her wits had scattered to the four winds. If Lady Cowper wished to do her an evil turn, she could have done no better than she had. But Fenella could not sit tongue-tied for the entire evening. She recalled Lady Cowper's remarks from last week.

''I understand you are recently back from the war. Will you return to the Peninsula?''

''No, I have sold out. I consider six years a sufficient time to spend in uncomfortable situations.'' He looked around at the assembly. The room was becoming crowded, and at a distance the violins were tuning up. "How often I thought of just such an evening as this!" he said, almost to himself. He glanced down at her. "Although, I must say, I had no precise idea of the lady I wished beside me. Now, of course, I do.''

Fenella, her wits gathered, deemed Mr. Thorne a touch too forward. "I suspect," she said pleasantly, "you found customs much more informal in Portugal. It is small wonder that you have got out of the way of things in London.''

He regarded her narrowly. "It seems I have. Very well, I make my apologies. But," he added, "will you not take pity on me and teach me how I should go on?''

He looked so meek that she smiled. "There is no need to humbug me, Mr. Thorne. I owe you much, if not my life, for your rescue of me in the storm. Of course, I shall be pleased to tell you anything you wish.'' Her eyes locked with his, and for a long moment she could not breathe. His gaze held warmth, amusement, and something else she could not identify. She hurried into speech. "The first thing, of course, is to move into company. We have been apart from the others too long.''

He rose and proffered his hand to assist her to her feet. "I shall not say, Miss Standish, what I might have said were you and I to meet in Portugal.''

She looked a question, but he shook his head. "I must be guided by your notions of propriety, you know.''

She was forced to enlighten him further. "I am betrothed, you know. To Gerald Lanceford.''

Mr. Thorne smiled gently. "For the moment, at least.''

He led her onto the floor to make up the dance set then forming, and the rest of the evening passed uneventfully.

Rumors fly swiftly, as a rule, and generally come quickly to the very ears one would wish to be deaf. The next afternoon saw Gerald Lanceford at Fenella's door, protest on his lips and a vague uneasiness in his heart.

His accusations of a lack of care on her part for his good name, escalating into a charge of outright infidelity, were a grave mistake, as was his remark as he turned to leave the room.

"When the full realization of your extreme lack of decorum comes to you, you may send for me," he said loftily. "After all, you are a betrothed woman!"

"For the moment," she agreed, realizing with momentary confusion that she was echoing Mr. Thorne's words of the previous evening. "But no longer, Gerald. Pray send the proper notice at once to the *Gazette*."

Stunned, seeing his farms whistled down the wind, he protested feebly, "You'll change your mind."

"Believe me, I shall not."

Within the next few days, Sir Giles, as was proper in a prudent father, took Mr. Thorne into his library, poured out a glass of port, offered him one of his best cigars, and bade him sit.

"What do they call you?"

"My full name is William Anscom Robert Thorne. Unfortunately, the initials spell a word, and I've been plagued from school days by the nickname Wart."

Sir Giles chuckled. "Related to old Lord Wolver, I believe?"

"My great-uncle," agreed Robert. "My grandfather was his younger brother."

"Not in line for the title, I assume?"

"I do not expect so. My cousin Gervase Sandys will inherit."

"The older Sandys boy was killed in the war, wasn't he? How about you? You're on leave?"

"No, I sold out. I was on the line with my regiment for three years, and on the general's staff for three."

Sir Giles poked the fire. "More port? I agree, wiser not to indulge. But you don't appear to have been wounded."

Robert reflected. His privacy meant much to him, but if he intended to wed Fenella, and he was certain he did, he recognized her father's right to the truth.

"Actually, I am fortunate that the evidence of my wounds can be covered by Scott's coats and this admirable new fashion of pantaloons. I daresay my left leg does not show to advantage in knee breeches!''

Sir Giles laughed. ''You don't limp, however?''

''Rainy weather or extreme fatigue, sir, will betray me.''

Sir Giles nodded. ''What about your brother?''

Robert was puzzled. ''I am an only child, sir.''

''Rudolph, I think his name is?''

''Rudolph, I thank God, is not my brother,'' said Robert from his heart. ''Son of my father's younger brother. I think he is abroad, although I confess the family does not interest itself overmuch in his whereabouts. He has nothing left of his inheritance, and I suspect he has pockets to let most of the time.''

''Abroad, eh? I thought I saw him . . . Ah, well, it is likely I would not recognize him now, since the last time I saw either of you properly you were both schoolboys, visiting Wolver. The old man keeps to himself these days, you know.''

''I visited him for a day, when I first came home,'' said Robert. ''He was so frail I did not stay, lest I tire him overmuch. But he was very good to me when I was younger.''

Thus Robert received Sir Giles's stamp of approval, and he pursued his wooing of Fenella. All went merrily along, and each day Robert became more enchanted with her.

Fenella danced, ate, drove in Hyde Park, went to the theater to see Sarah Siddons, and did not know what she was doing. She seemed to exist in a cloud of rosy hue, populated by two persons only, and she was content to look no further.

Robert, however, had long been a man of acumen and action. He noticed, at last, that even though he was prepared to do battle for Fenella, there was little enough competition standing in his way, even after the notice of her broken betrothal appeared in the *Gazette*. Discreet questioning of his man of affairs revealed that Miss Standish, while exceedingly well-bred and of excellent family, was possessed of little fortune.

''Sir Giles inherited an encumbered estate,'' Robert was told. ''He's managing now, and if he has another five years or so, he can set all to rights again. But he cannot summon up a dowry. . . ."

And since Robert had no need of an addition to his fortune, which was more than adequate for his needs, he saw no obstacle in his way to prevent his securing the bride he wanted.

Several days after his enlightening interview with his man of business, Robert brought Fenella home from a party at Holland House. His intention was to escort her into the house, request an interview the next morning with Sir Giles, and then, given permission to pay his addresses, make his offer to Fenella.

Robert glanced at Fenella, sitting in the corner of the coach. "Tired?" he asked gently.

She nodded. "I'll probably not open my eyes until midday tomorrow!"

"I wish I could watch you—" Catching sight of her expression, he stopped short, with a laugh. "My apologies. This is London, not Portugal!"

She smiled. "You have made such sensational progress, Mr. Thorne! I must hire myself out as an instructress to returning soldiers—teach them civilized ways again!"

"I warn you, I shall not stand and serve as an example for you to point to!" After a moment, he said on a plaintive note, "Can you not bring yourself to call me Robert?"

She was amused. "Did I not hear one of your old friends call you by quite another name?"

With mock severity he told her, "I have made a resolve to *call out* anyone using that outrageous nickname! Those . . . important to me call me Robert."

"Very well, I am suitably impressed . . . Robert!"

He nearly spoke his mind then, but the coach slowed to turn into the square and the opportunity was lost.

They pulled up before the house, and Fenella gasped. "What is it? Something's amiss!"

The house was lit from top to bottom, and the front door stood open, light spilling out onto the steps. From the street she could see people within scurrying about in an agitated fashion.

Sir Giles came hastily from the back of the hall when Fenella stepped inside, Robert behind her.

"Word's come from Oakhurst," he said briefly. "We're leaving at first light."

"Word!" cried Fenella. "Word about what?"

"I'll tell you on the way. Best get packed at once."

"Is there any way, sir, I may be of service?" asked Robert.

Sir Giles looked thoughtfully at him. "I don't believe so, at least just now. But come down sometime if you wish. You'll be welcome." He nodded to him, and went into the library, closing the door behind him.

Fenella looked up at Robert. "I am so sorry to leave London."

His voice was tender. "May I come down to Oakhurst?"

"Please do."

"I should not wish to intrude on whatever urgent matter has come up. Perhaps in a sennight?"

She nodded. He lifted her hand to his lips and said a soft good-night.

She watched him drive away before she turned to her maid and went upstairs to direct her packing.

3

The southern coast of England, in that year of 1811, was a troubled coast. Fairly close across the waters lay an always dangerous and greedy Napolean Bonaparte, and the strong westerly gales sweeping up the Channel from the Atlantic, so it was said, were the only protection available against an invasion.

The westerlies and the British Navy kept the Channel free of French landing craft. However, even in the most perilous times, small swift craft set out for the French coast to bring back casks of brandy, casks of geneva and of rum, as well as tobacco, wine, and tea.

The smuggling trade had been a mainstay of the local economy as long as there had been customs officers to outwit. Now, with so many revenue cutters commandeered by the Navy, the illicit traffic flourished. Usually the smugglers confined their quarrels to their natural enemies, the excise men. But once in a while a hapless innocent found himself intruding where he should not.

One such luckless lad, young Brumm, was the son of one of Sir Giles's tenants. Sir Giles, rightly outraged, had sought to learn the identity of the killer, but with the passage of months the trail grew cold, and Sir Giles at last recognized the futility of his quest.

But, wondered Fenella, if not some new clue which might lead to the killer, what could have brought Sir Giles back posthaste to Oakhurst?

Oakhurst stood on a height overlooking the bay, not far

from Lyme Regis, where the Duke of Monmouth, pretender to the English throne, had landed a century and more since. The house itself was comfortable and spacious, built of Dorset stone in a style that offered welcome and warmth rather than elegance and fashion.

Two days after their hurried return from London, Fenella stood at one of the tall narrow windows facing the broad bay. The London Season in which she had been engrossed only a few days ago seemed unbelievably distant. If she stepped outside onto the broad terrace now, instead of the hoots and cries, the rumble of wheels, that were constantly heard in London, she would hear only the sea breeze rustling in the ancient oaks and, far off, the bleating of sheep in the inland fields.

It was so good to be home again! she thought. She could almost forget her father's anxious frown, nearly constant these last few days.

As always, when the Standishes were in residence at Oakhurst, Fenella's old governess, now regarded in the role of companion, came from home in Taunton to keep her company. Fenella could see at this moment Miss Waite taking her daily exercise on the terrace. Not for anything short of disaster would she step onto the lawns, considering green grass as always damp, contact with it leading inevitably to a congestion on the chest.

A stranger, watching Fenella, would not have considered her a great beauty in the fashion of the time, but she had her own charms. Her mouth was too large, but she smiled often and revealed generosity and good humor. Her hair was of deep auburn, with fiery points of flame when the sun shone on it.

But her eyes were her best feature, she had been told. They were gray, dark as the bay when she was in a temper, clear and calm when she was happy.

And she was happy, excessively happy—for Robert had promised to come down in a week's time, and already two days had passed since they had left London! And, she thought very privately, his eagerness to visit her home, and the warm light in his eyes, could mean only one thing. How could she ever have considered Gerald Lanceford?

Sir Giles quietly entered the room. "Fenella?" He joined her at the window.

She looked up at him. A spare man, still with a full head of graying hair, a little stooped with his years. But his gray eyes, so like Fenella's, still held a twinkle upon occasion, and even at the worst of times they reflected a fundamental kindness.

"Sorry to be home again?" he asked.

"Of course not, Papa. In fact, I do not know how I shall bring myself to leave again."

He took her hand and caressed her fingers. "I recall," he said slowly, "when your whole hand fit neatly into my palm."

His somber mood was contagious. At length Fenella ventured, "Papa, what is it? Have you found out who murdered young Brumm?"

He gave a start. Without meeting her eyes, he said, "How . . . that is, why would you think such a thing?"

"Why else," persisted his daughter, "would you need to rush back here, saying urgent matters had come up? I thought you had given up the search for the villain who fired the shot?"

"Not given up, my dear. I should never give up."

"I cannot but feel it is dangerous for you."

He sighed. "Do not worry about it, Fenella. The trail is very cold."

"Then, if it is not that, why do you not trust me? What is the matter?"

"Nothing, child."

"Papa, don't try to cozen me," she said, with an attempt at playfulness. "You know I shall discover all your secrets in time." An incident of the morning came to her. "That letter from Baldwin! That is what has put you in such a mood!"

The letter from Sir Giles's agent in London had arrived that very morning, and her father had taken it into his study to read, closing the door behind him. Since this reticence had become his regular practice in the last couple of years, she had not paid particular heed. But now her father's odd manner aroused misgivings in her.

"You've heard something unpleasant about Mr. Thorne!"

"No, my dear. If I had, I should have forbidden him the house at once." He continued in a thoughtful vein. "I shall be extremely glad to see you settled."

Miss Waite, her day's exercise accomplished, joined them then, and the conversation turned general. Soon Sir Giles made his excuses and left them, but Fenella's uneasiness persisted for some time.

Miss Waite was no fool. She had guided her motherless charge through the intricacies of acquiring solid knowledge, as well as elegance of manners. Being something of a bluestocking, she did not subscribe to the general idea that young females should be given only such knowledge as would make them agreeable to gentlemen, so Fenella's education was broader than that of most young ladies.

The newly published *Mangnall's Historical and Miscellaneous Questions for the Use of Young People* was swiftly left behind and Fenella moved on to history, French, and even a smattering of Greek and Latin.

Miss Waite presumed, therefore, on their long intimacy to inquire into the cause of her young friend's lack of her ordinary high spirits.

"I am aware that I interrupted your conversation with your papa," she said delicately. "I hope nothing is amiss."

After a moment Fenella answered, "I do not think so."

She glanced at Miss Waite with the smile that had won that lady's heart at the very first, before she came to know her better and valued her for her sweetness of disposition, her bright intelligence, and the wry humor that emerged at unexpected moments.

"It seems almost that my father wishes to be rid of me!"

"Of course you cannot be serious, my dear," said Miss Waite with affection.

It was later that day that the mystery that surrounded Sir Giles's abrupt departure from London, and his unwonted somberness since their return to Oakhurst, grew even deeper.

Fenella and Miss Waite sat comfortably in the salon, Fenella's embroidery forgotten in her lap as Miss Waite took them both into a world of romance in the Trossachs valley of Scotland.

Sir Giles stood just inside the door, unnoticed for a few minutes. When she caught sight of him, Miss Waite blushed. "I am reading dear Sir Walter's new poem," she explained, *"The Lady of the Lake."*

Then, seeing a polite dismissal in Sir Giles's expression, she tactfully left Fenella and her father, and went out to the broad terrace, where she could look out across the bay toward the western sky. If she were not mistaken—and her years of living on this height above the bay ensured that she was not likely to be wrong—a change in the weather was on the way.

The darkening sky had not reached the shade of purple that meant a storm was even now raging on the high moors to the west, but a smoke-blue haze veiled the afternoon sun. Probably another four or five hours, Miss Waite, a country-woman to her bones, calculated.

She would have been troubled, having more experience of the world than Fenella, had she been aware of the overtones in the conversation ending at that moment in the salon she had just quit.

Before Sir Giles left the salon he gave Fenella a small volume. "My dear," he said without apparent emotion, "I want you to have this. I fear I have not seen well to your upbringing, but perhaps this will make up for my derelictions."

Fenella looked at the package in her hands. "A Bible? But, Papa, I do have one of my own, and I am sure there are others in the library!"

"But I want you to keep this one. It belonged to my father, and has some sentimental value." So saying, he smiled and went through the foyer to the outer door, this man who had been dearest in all the world to her, long before Robert had secured his own place in her heart. He turned as though to add a final word, but said nothing. Before he continued down the steps, he turned and waved.

Fenella hurried to the door. Her father had joined Stone, the boatman, and the two set off down the drive together.

Partway down the drive a well-trodden path turned off to
the right, a path which led down the hill to where Sir Giles's
sailboat was moored. She knew the two men were masterly
sailors, so there was no reason for her to feel any concern
for them.

However, even though at this moment Fenella was standing
in the warm hazy sunlight, unaccountably she shivered.

"Only a short sail," Sir Giles had assured her. "I'll be
back within the hour."

Fenella, for no reason she recognized, sat down on the
entrance-porch steps to wait.

Sir Giles did not return within the hour.

When Stone, the boatman, came to her some two hours
later, Sir Giles had still not returned. Fenella looked up at
Stone with a smile of relief.

"At last you two are back! I've been anxious . . ."

His expression did not reassure her. "Isn't Sir Giles
back?"

"No," she said, "of course not. You were with him. You
know . . ." Seeing a frown darkening his features, she stood
up quickly.

He shook his head. "Sir Giles wished to go alone." He
answered her unspoken question. "Why, miss? He didn't
say. But I did wonder . . ."

He cast a look out across the water. The sky had turned
a pale milky blue hue, and the ominous cloud bank was
climbing fast toward the zenith. "Sure he can read the
weather as well as anybody," Stone continued in an attempt
to soothe Fenella. "Sir Giles knows what he is doing."

Fenella, still seeing in her mind her father's farewell as
clearly as though he stood before her at this moment, could
not be comforted. "I know something is wrong, Stone."

"Now, miss, it's not late yet."

"He said within the hour."

Seeing that Fenella was truly worried, he offered, "I'll
go down to the wharf, miss. He may already be coming
ashore."

"I've been watching," said Fenella. "I'd see him, I
think."

"Mebbe he ran to cover in another cove, or even in Lyme Regis. It looks bad enough, I agree, but it'll be all of an hour before the storm breaks. Not to worry, miss."

Reluctantly conceding that Stone was in all likelihood correct, that Sir Giles, seeing the storm coming, might well have chosen to run to shore without trying to make his own anchorage, she followed the boatman down the steep path that led to the boathouse and the small pier stretching out into the water of the cove.

Down at the level of the water, the sweep of the bay seemed vast as the Channel itself. Cat's-paws of wind picked up little ripples, sure sign of gales to come. Across the broad expanse scuttled small boats, all of them larger than Sir Giles's sailboat, and all of them clearly making speedily for safety.

Fenella's good sense told her that her father was a thoroughly experienced seaman. There was no need to worry. But she could not shake the feeling that gripped her.

No boat the size of Sir Giles's was in sight. Larger waves were now beginning to kick up, but even though the *Sprite*'s hull might be hidden in the trough, the sail should be visible.

She closed her eyes to shut out the sight of the water, and stepped back, bumping into Miss Waite, who had joined them quietly.

"You are worried too," exclaimed Fenella. Then, after a moment, she was able to put her fears into words. "Stone, do you really think he is all right? Or should we . . . ?"

"Yes, Miss Fenella," Stone said, answering the question that had not been spoken. His eyes strayed to Miss Waite, and a message of understanding passed between them.

"Miss Fenella, shall I notify the Coast Guard?" Upon her reluctant nod, Stone disappeared.

Miss Waite put her arm around Fenella's shoulders and spoke softly. "Come, my dear, we can do no good here." She did not precisely know why she was convinced that trouble lay in wait just ahead. She only knew that Sir Giles had had something on his mind since he returned from London. And in her experience, when a gentleman began to behave oddly, trouble was not far behind.

Calling in the customs seemed to Fenella almost to

pronounce Sir Giles as already dead. She knew in her bones that her father would not return. Those long hours that stretched after Miss Waite had urged her back to the house, to endure till the outcome, were endless.

The servants, cowed by Summers, the butler, tiptoed around as though the mourning hatchment were already over the entrance. At some point, Miss Waite sent for refreshments, both to restore Fenella and to give the anxious servants something to do.

"There's no news, my dear," Miss Waite pointed out, breaking into a brooding silence, "and as long as there is none, then there is no reason to expect that when it does come, it will be unpleasant."

It all made good sense, thought Fenella, but she could not believe it. What were the customs men doing? Why hadn't they found him? How she longed for Robert's good sense, his comforting shoulder!

But at last the waiting was over. The sound of wheels on the drive roused them all, and Fenella reached the salon door just as the butler opened the great entrance door.

Three men came tentatively into the foyer, water streaming from their coats onto the black-and-white tiled floor.

All were dressed in rugged all-weather gear, and it was clear that the storm had struck, even if those in the salon had not been aware of the thunder and the streaming rain on the windows.

Fenella felt the blood drain from her face. Her mouth opened but she could not speak.

"Miss Standish?" said the one who appeared to be the leader. "I fear I have bad news."

"You have not found him?"

It never became an easy duty, thought the official, no matter how many tragedies he had had to announce to shocked kinfolk.

The tiny flame of hope that Fenella had nurtured all through the past hours wavered as she read the coastguardsman's expression, and then went out for good.

Sir Giles Standish had been found. He was lying in the bottom of his sailboat, the mast broken and the sail, still attached, limp in the water. The boat had been urged gently by the waves until it came gently to shore in a cove a mile or so down the coast.

Sir Giles was dead.

"Why didn't he come ashore? Was he ill? Did he have a seizure and lie unconscious for an hour or so? Why didn't I go with him?"

Miss Waite answered all the questions, but to no avail, for Fenella simply asked them again. At length the doctor came, with his drafts and brisk commands, and she was put to bed.

When she awoke to the gray daylight of continuing storm, she knew that her life had been altered past any recognition.

4

Although no one could replace her father, what was done was done. The mystery surrounding the reason for his fatal accident, and even the details of how it happened, would most likely never come to light.

But the next day, Mr. Forsyth, the doctor who had brought Fenella into the world and recently had seen her father out, drove up to the entrance of Oakhurst. He seemed reluctant to descend, but noticing an assistant groom waiting at the horse's head, he gave a huge sigh and left the vehicle.

Fenella was glad to see him. Miss Waite was somewhere in the house making rooms ready for the expected arrival from London of Mr. Baldwin, her father's man of business.

Therefore, Fenella unfortunately was alone when the doctor revealed his errand.

After greetings were exchanged, he said in a grave tone of voice, "I'm sorry to tell you, Fenella, but—" He broke off, then said uneasily, "I do wish Miss Waite were present."

Now thoroughly alarmed, Fenella cried, "What is it? Pray tell me, sir. I am not one of these die-away young misses!"

She wished, after he had begun to speak, that she had been less brave. Mr. Forsyth's news stunned her.

The body of Sir Giles, when it came time to bury him, was washed carefully, and to the surprise of the undertaker, who at once called the authorities, it was discovered that there was a bullet hole in the temple, until now hidden by heavy graying hair.

"Murdered!" exclaimed Fenella.

The doctor shook his head mournfully. "Sorry, my dear, but it looks to us as if he took his own life."

There was no way that Fenella would believe that her father had committed suicide. There was no lack of arguments, respectful but obstinate, given her by the messenger and designed to convince her.

But she remembered that odd note in her father's voice just as he left her for the last time. Maybe he *had* done away with himself. But why?

There were so many questions, and no answers. Thoughts tumbled like squirrels in a cage, or, especially in the night hours, with leaden feet like oxen at a treadmill.

What was she to do?

Fenella counted the days till Robert would come. When the seventh day passed into history, she felt as though she had been marooned in the South Pacific. Suppose that were the case—she could not feel more alone than she did at this moment.

Miss Waite was comforting and bracing by turns. Fenella seemed to sink more deeply into her well of grief, and Miss Waite began to entertain serious doubt about Fenella's full recovery.

Fenella had taken Miss Waite into her confidence about her expectations of Robert. But he was already a day late. Where was he?

At that moment, Robert Thorne was tooling down the road leading to Oakhurst, in a light curricle, baggage for a week loaded on at the back. Mr. Thorne, having had vast experience with baggage wagons and their tendency never to be where they were most needed, had learned to travel lightly.

Oram, his groom and former batman, stole a glance at him and suppressed a grin. The colonel was well on the way to being leg-shackled, he reckoned, and about time, too. Miss Standish was a taking young lady, and Oram was heartily in favor of the match.

The June day was fine, without a cloud in the sky. Robert could not discern any cloud to mar his own future, either, since he believed he knew Fenella's affections to be his. Within a sennight, his optimistic nature told him, Fenella would be his own, the announcement on its way to the *Gazette,* and the wedding festivities in full swing!

His only doubt, as he drove up the winding driveway to the entrance of Oakhurst, was whether he could persuade his lady to forgo the waiting and to marry him by special license.

Within an hour, his rosy optimism had been routed, and doubts crowded in on him like Portuguese guerrillas out of ambush.

The first intimation of change came when he caught sight of the mourning hatchment above the door.

Please, God, not Fenella!

Not Fenella, he thought with unspeakable relief. An hour later, he had been placed by Fenella and Miss Waite in possession of the facts and mysteries surrounding the tragedy.

How he wished he had spoken to Sir Giles before they had left London! Now he dared not press her too urgently. He must respect her grief, at least till the worst of it was past.

Now that Robert had come, Fenella's spirits began to rise. Miss Waite regarded Mr. Thorne with favor. The best thing, she thought, would be for the wedding to take place at once, very quietly, forgetting any period of mourning. This situation—since Fenella had no relatives to be of service to her— was so desperate that to wait upon convention could only be harmful. Miss Waite believed that the worst was over.

She was wrong.

There was no reason, Robert believed, for Sir Giles to take his own life. Surely he would have waited, supposing his financial situation to be worse than was known, until his only daughter was settled?

Convincing reason enough arrived with Sir Giles's London agent, Mr. Baldwin.

"If you have bad news," said Fenella, "I should like Miss Waite and Mr. Thorne to be present."

Fenella could not later remember the long, prosy

explanation that Mr. Baldwin was at pains to give her. "That letter I sent your father only last week explained it all." Loans that could not be repaid, and the money could be counted as lost, unsound purchases of household goods by Sir Giles's father, leaving little working capital—"whatever that may be," thought Fenella. And crops that failed, and livestock that died . . .

The whole sorry story was that of a once prosperous estate that had fallen on evil times.

"We have been compounding with creditors, attempting to put together a dowry sufficient to suit . . ." He fell silent. He had not meant to confide Sir Giles's worries to his daughter, and belatedly he recalled that Mr. Thorne, now sitting opposite him, was not the fiancé who had been so demanding.

In another vein he continued, "I tried, Miss Fenella, but I could not even arrange a modest allowance for you."

There was utter silence as he finished. At length, Robert cleared his throat and ventured, "Then Miss Standish is without funds?"

Mr. Baldwin, for once in his life, allowed himself the luxury of leaping to a conclusion. "She is, as I have tried to convey, without funds of any kind. The farms will be sold and the house and its furnishings will be in the hands of the bailiffs by week's end. But of course, Miss Standish will not be derelict, since she is to marry you?"

Robert stiffened, dismayed. Had the entire world known he wanted to marry Fenella? He did and he would, but he wished to manage his offer in his own way and in what he considered to be the best time.

But Miss Waite observed his sudden stillness, misread it, and began to consider plans for Miss Standish, spinster, for it seemed clear to her that Fenella was not destined to be Mrs. Thorne.

Fenella sank back into her chair and closed her eyes. Not only was Papa gone, an irrevocable loss, but also the estate was gone. Now she knew why Papa had gone out that day with a deeply sad expression in his eyes. He intended even then to find a way out of his troubles, but she could not,

even now, with Baldwin watching her with compassion, and
knowing that the bailiffs were not far behind—not even now
could she believe that Papa knew he was leaving his only
child to face the troubles that he himself could not.

But it was so. Baldwin was the soul of honesty, and besides
that, he had brought proof of Papa's enormous debts. She
was not only an orphan—she was a pauper.

By noon the next day she had at least understood what must
next happen. Mr. Baldwin had told the servants, and held
a long conference with the farm agent.

Later, the moment came. Not the moment that Robert
would have chosen, but the one that necessity, never a
respecter of romance, required.

Alone with Fenella, Robert made his offer. "Will you do
me the great honor of becoming my wife?"

She did not answer. Instead, she moved to the window and
stood with her back to him. He was moved to further speech.
"I will arrange for a special license, and we may be wed
before—"

"Before I must be married from an empty house?
Moreover, a house that is not mine? How would that look?"

He did not find the edge in her voice to be reassuring.

"Of course, if you do not wish it . . . I know this is not
the best time to tell you my feelings."

"No," she said so faintly he thought he must be mistaken.

"You must have been aware of my regard."

Movement outside the window caught her eye. Along the
drive where it curved from the stables to join the main sweep
before the door, walked a man leading two horses—one the
black gelding called Caesar, and the other her own sorrel
mare, Amber. So many times she and her father had ridden
together on those horses—days now gone forever.

Grief thickened her throat, pride stiffened her shoulders,
and led her to say, "You will not wish to wed a penniless
orphan, Mr. Thorne. Do not feel you must offer for me."

"I *have* offered. And you will allow me my own counsel
as to the lady I wish to marry." After a moment he continued,
"It is much the best thing for you to do."

Had he swooped her up in his arms at that moment and

covered her face and hair with kisses, he might have prevailed. But in his wish not to press her too much, he kept his desires under rigid control. In his gravity, the gallant who had won her heart in London was lost, and she did not recognize the man standing before her.

"The best thing for me?" she echoed. "But not for you, is that your meaning? I do understand you, sir. And believe me, I am duly cognizant of the great honor you have paid me in asking me to be your wife—I think this is the correct response?—but I shall never accept your offer. Our minds on this head are poles apart."

She was daunted to see that Robert had turned ashen. "You think I offered from *duty*?"

Through rigid lips she answered, "I beg you to say no more. My mind is resolved."

His eyes dark in his pale face, he watched her for a few moments. He perceived in her no sign of relenting, and at last, without a word, he turned and left.

He was not resigned to failure, however, and the next days he called, only to be refused by Summers. Miss Waite, too, was not available, since she had seen what she believed was shock when he learned that dear Fenella was bankrupt.

His thoughts were totally overset. He had thought she liked him, was well on the way to loving him—and he was mistaken. He supposed he would someday recover, but it would not be easy to give his heart away again.

Fenella, on the other hand, did not look to the future, for all she saw there was dreary desolation. Papa gone, and Robert gone, and although she could have had Robert for the lifting of a finger, she would never know whether he loved her or was simply a man of honor. He had certainly given the impression that he was interested in her, but she had not missed that involuntary reaction when Mr. Baldwin had laid out her situation.

She was much relieved now that she had resolved the question of Robert—certainly she was!

At last it came down to the last few moments Fenella would ever spend at Oakhurst. Her farewells to the servants had been said. The bailiffs' men were carrying out the furniture. She had no more tears left.

She sat on a chair in the tiled foyer, watching all the mementos of her life pass physically before her. Finally the chair in which she sat was demanded.

But she still had in her hands the last tangible possession of the past—her father's Bible.

5

Fenella walked through the house one last time. She had once taken pleasure in the thought that Robert would be at her side as she left her home—upon her marriage, of course.

But she had sent him away—and he had gone. She had guessed correctly: he had offered for her only out of a sense of duty. Had his motives been otherwise, he would have overcome all her objections and insisted that they be married at once.

And she would not now be only a shell filled with a lonely desolation.

Fenella thrust all the might-have-beens away in the dustbin of her memories, and vowed not to take them out again. Perhaps she might bring them to light when the hurt had eased. Say, in thirty years!

Fenella and Miss Waite traveled to the governess's home in Taunton in the bailiffs' carriage. They met few vehicles on their way, and if Fenella particularly noticed one of them, a curricle driven toward Oakhurst by a man she knew, she gave no sign of recognition.

Stunned, Robert—intending to try once again with Fenella—turned his vehicle in the roadway. So, it was all over. Her deliberate snub convinced him. She did not want him.

"You're welcome to stay with me, my dear, as long as you wish. I shall be glad of your company."

"But I cannot stay forever!" Fenella gave a great sigh. "I must begin to earn my living."

Sir Giles would not have approved of his daughter's seeking gainful employment, thought Miss Waite, remembering that proud and honorable gentleman. But he was not here to object, nor had he provided an alternative.

"Is there no relation on whom you might call to come to your aid?"

"No one. Save an ancient cousin in Scotland. I am not even sure of her name."

"Do I not remember correctly that the Earl of Wolver was a great friend of your father's?"

Fenella forced herself to be patient with her dear friend —her *only* friend, as it happened. "Lord Wolver has been an invalid these twenty years. Even though his estates adjoined ours—or what used to be ours—I never met him. His grandson is with the army in Spain, I believe."

"Oh, dear," said Miss Waite. "I do hope he comes back safely. It is such a shame to see the old families die out because of that dreadful Bonaparte man."

After a week during which Fenella stayed closed up in the small cottage, Miss Waite judged it to be the right time to urge Fenella to move beyond her deep grief. Breakfast, a time when one faces a day full of possibilities, and one has been restored by excellent ham and biscuits and strong tea, was Miss Waite's favorite hour for giving bracing advice.

"Now, my dear . . ." she began.

Unexpectedly, Fenella laughed. "You are about to scold me, are you not? I recognize that same note in your voice that always spurred me to examine my conscience."

Gratified by Fenella's response, and perceiving it to be a sign that the girl was over the worst of her grief, Miss Waite spoke her approval. "Sir Giles would not wish you to mourn him forever, you know."

Fenella's expression altered. "Papa? I will miss him until I die. I believe I am as angry as I have ever been!"

Aghast, Miss Waite whispered, "At your father? Oh, Fenella, that is very wrong of you!"

"No, not at Papa. How could I be? But I tell you now,

Drusilla Waite, that I do not take kindly to being considered merely a dowry and nothing more. Offering only because he had been paying distinguishing attention to me for a month or more! It was easy enough to see the shock when Mr. Baldwin explained all to him. Drusilla Waite, I promise you no man will ever again be in a position to do as much to me! Never!''

Miss Waite could not quarrel with Fenella's conclusion.

"Dear Drusilla," Fenella went on, "you have been such a support to me. I believe I'm ready to leave this cocoon I've made out of your cottage. Have you any errands I might do?"

It was unfortunate that, having made an enormous effort to ease her hostess's worries about herself, to cast off the dreary thoughts that had engulfed her, and ventured forth into the streets of Taunton, she should have sustained another unexpected blow.

Fenella had not yet come to the realization of her altered circumstances. Now, as she passed St. Mary's Church, she paused to look up at the strong and awe-inspiring facade of the building, a perfect example of Perpendicular style. At length she tore her gaze away and started again on her way.

Ahead of her was a woman she recognized. Lady Worter, an old friend of Lady Standish's, had emerged from her carriage stopped before the vicarage gate, and stood hesitant on the pavement. It was clear that she recognized Fenella, for she stood and looked for a long moment. Fenella's face lit in response, and then, deliberately, Lady Worter turned away and entered the vicarage grounds.

Fenella was nearly home before she was calm enough to think. Lady Worter had administered an unmistakable cut. It was beyond belief!

No one had ever snubbed Fenella before. But, with a sinking coldness at the pit of her stomach, she realized that this would not be the only snub. Nothing could have made her more aware of her situation, outside the boundaries of society, than Lady Worter. Fenella recalled that in her childhood she had called her Lady Warthog. The memory did not help.

She had lost everything—Papa, Gerald, her home, any kind of income, even any future she could recognize.

She entered the house with, creditably, a firm step and an appearance of cheerfulness, and announced, "Drusilla, you must teach me to be a governess!"

"An employer will demand of a governess 'unimpeachable morality, a mild and cheerful temper, and an obliging disposition.' I am quoting, of course."

Miss Waite took her responsibilities seriously. Fenella would have more than one moment of disillusion even if she were the most fortunate governess alive. At least Miss Waite could prepare her.

"You must forget, dear child, that you were ever Miss Standish of Oakhurst. It is not the thing, you know, for the governess to outrank the lady of the house."

Fenella murmured understanding. "But what do you mean by 'an obliging disposition'?"

"You may find that a nursemaid may be required at times. Or you may be invited to spend your leisure time mending linens."

"I shall simply refuse." Miss Waite frowned. "Oh, I see. That is what you mean by forgetting who I am—was. Well, if I must, I must. I do see there is more to it than simply saying, 'Mary, today you will master natural philosophy.' "

Miss Waite chuckled. "And do not forget to pretend ignorance of mathematics. That is not a fit subject for young ladies."

"I shall not have to pretend. Perhaps I would have understood Papa's troubles better had I been educated along those lines. Not that Papa would have allowed you to teach me, I know. But I might have been of some help to him."

Miss Waite laid her hand on Fenella's in a comforting little gesture, and then continued her instructions.

"You may count yourself fortunate if you gain employment in a house with no young gentlemen."

"Why is that?"

"Young gentlemen have a propensity for making trouble with the housemaids, and many feel a governess, being also unprotected, is a fair object for their games. A kiss behind the door is the least of what may be expected, and very often worse."

Fenella leaned forward, fascinated. "Did any of that happen to you?"

Miss Waite blushed deeply. "Let us get on with your lessons, Fenella. I know you disliked *Mangnall's,* but you will find the questions in that book of great value . . ."

Some six months later, Fenella, her education at the hands of Miss Waite completed, undertook her first teaching position.

Her surroundings, in the home of a prosperous Bristol merchant with social ambitions, bore no resemblance to Oakhurst. This house was furnished in the latest—and, to Fenella, the ugliest—new fashions. Mr. Hervey was gone on business all day, and his wife read novels and petted her three King Charles spaniels until the hour of her husband's homecoming approached. Then with the help of her maid she emerged to dress for dinner, at the same time giving the indelible impression that she was exhausted from the many household duties that gave her no respite.

Although Fenella was amused at Mrs. Hervey and her foibles, there was no one with whom to share her enjoyment, and she turned her attention to her charges. There were three children, barely out of the nursery, and all in need of learning their letters.

Fenella was the first governess ever employed in the Hervey household, and the family was not quite sure how to deal with her. Mrs. Hervey seemed to feel that Fenella's status was somewhere between a personal maid who ate in the kitchen (although Fenella, mindful of Miss Waite's words of wisdom, always asked for a tray in her room) and an honored guest who joined the family at dinner. Mr. Hervey's thoughts about her were sometimes excessively and unpleasantly clear.

Although her life was not as it had been, yet she had very little to complain of. She was too busy to think overmuch about Robert, and when she did, she was gratified to discover that he was beginning to fade. She could no longer, without an effort, bring his features to mind.

But sometimes, when she woke with a start as the faint light of dawn turned the world into a gray mist, she was crying, and she knew she had been dreaming of home.

At first, she dreamed much about Oakhurst, about Papa, about the clothes and jewels and books she had had, her furs and her own carriage. But as time went on, the dream faded, as though her dreaming mind understood that those things were gone, were done with.

But then, why did she dream about Robert? Not precisely about him, she corrected herself, but often about the nightmare when the vivid lightning lit up the skies and drove the horses mad. That dream always began with Robert rescuing her—as he had in fact delivered her from danger—but his identity altered and in the unaccountable way of dreams, his features changed and became those of a stranger. At that point she always awoke.

She was happy enough with the ordinary, unaccomplished, good-natured Hervey children.

Happy enough, that is, until the day of the dinner party when Fenella had held her first post for nearly ten months.

Mrs. Hervey was entertaining those of her acquaintance who lived nearby. The dinner was elaborate to a fault, and the guests were to stay overnight rather than chancing the roads by moonlight.

The first-comers had arrived and were taking refreshment in the salon. Fenella often made up a place at the table when there were just the family at table, or at best a few guests. However, on this occasion Mrs. Hervey had not informed Fenella of her wishes.

Fenella slipped down the stairs. She had not dressed for dinner, but she thought it advisable to inquire whether she were wanted. There were no servants in the foyer at the moment, and Fenella moved toward the open door into the large salon.

Mrs. Hervey's ill-bred voice was raised. The shrillness of it carried clearly and well across the room and into the hall, when Fenella paused for a moment. As she heard her employer's remarks, she knew she must retreat up the stairs at once. She could not afford to be caught in such a compromising situation. But she was gripped by what she heard through the open door.

"Oh, yes," Mrs. Hervey was saying, "it's the same Miss Standish. I recall how I saw her once when we traveled to London. Driving a phaeton and pair in Hyde Park, she was, with her groom up fancy as you please behind. It's against nature for a lady to drive herself. I know Mr. Hervey would not approve."

There was a murmur, and then Mrs. Hervey's voice rose again. "Miss High-and-Mighty, she was then." She tittererd. "I guess we all know now who's holding the reins!"

Fenellal hardly knew how she got up the stairs. She had been humiliated before, particularly by Lady Worter, but even that had not stung as badly as the malicious contempt displayed by a woman she had never harmed.

In the morning her small trunk was packed and corded, ready for the carter. Her final interview with Mrs. Hervey was not a happy one for the latter, for on this occasion Fenella had not spoken as a governess, but as the well-bred and even arrogant Miss Standish of Oakhurst.

She had ample time over the next several months, Fenella found, to regret her quixotic behavior. A position as governess was not overly difficult to find. However, employers who wished to trust a young lady of some presence and near-beauty in a household of susceptible male juveniles of an inquiring mind were thin on the ground, nor would she have accepted a post of this kind.

She had learned economies over the months since her father's death. But her remaining coins were few, and she realized that she must accept the very next post offered to her.

6

At last, two years to the day after her departure from Oakhurst, a household of female children found themselves in need of Fenella's talents, and she traveled to a house near Epperstone in Nottinghamshire.

Chantrey Manor was a comfortable building of some size. Built for protection against the savage winter winds of this part of England, it was three stories of solid stone.

The sole male in the household was Sir Eustace Fletcher, some seventy years old, whose years had not mellowed his irascible disposition.

His only son had been killed in the Peninsular Wars, and Sir Eustace contrived to believe that his daughter-in-law, Sophy, had in some way been responsible for his death.

For her part, Sophy was the very picture of a downtrodden female, without intelligence and without resources. And yet, thought Fenella after she had been in residence for six months, it was instructive to ferret out in what hidden ways Sophy had managed to make a most comfortable life for herself and her daughters.

The daughters, of course, were Fenella's main charge. The elder, Charlotte, was eighteen, and in need of no guidance, in her own opinion. However, her mother, having a commendable wish to do her best for her children, believed that Fenella could so instruct Charlotte in decorum and the ways of society as to make her a credit to her mother.

The younger, Emma, was only eleven, and in Fenella's

judgment had had so little instruction as to be a clean slate on which to write.

"I do hope you are not going to be like the others," said Sophy in their first interview.

"The others?" echoed the new governess.

"All of them left. Not six months before they decided this was too isolated. London was the place for them, they said. And they are quite right. It may be that we ourselves will go to London." Then, with a quick look as though she had said more than she should have, she added, "Someday, of course. After all, I have two daughters to marry."

With her own recollection of London society in her mind, Fenella thought that to set Charlotte loose in the *ton* would lead to her immediate destruction.

"Of course, Mrs. Fletcher," said Fenella submissively.

London was never mentioned again. After six months, Fenella believed herself content. Her own room was spacious and comfortable, the fires generous, the fare ample and very palatable, and she had already received the twenty-five pounds she was due as a semiannual wage. My goodness, she thought, I have spent more than this in an hour on ribbons!

At last Robert was fading from her mind, and almost never intruded in her dreams. "I must not have loved him," she told herself stoutly, "and certainly he didn't love me. Only my fortune—well, that is gone and so is Robert, and of the two I regret only the fortune!"

Oakhurst and her own past might well have stayed in the limbo to which she had driven them, had not a sharp reminder come unexpectedly to her.

The nearest house to the west of Chantrey Manor belonged to a family named Pruitt. Sophy's artless gossip had informed Fenella that Mr. Pruitt was a wealthy and kind man, of no particular family, but his wife was exceedingly wellborn, and had married for love.

"In her case it turned out well," said Sophy. "There's money there, and their Fanny will likely have her pick when it comes time to marry. I wish . . ."

Mrs. Pruitt indeed seemed a happy woman. Fanny was far from entering the marriage market, since she was only a year older than Emma. As Sophy and her party entered Mrs. Pruitt's small parlor, Fenella was aware of a young man already calling on Mrs. Pruitt, and started when she heard his name.

Dolph Thorne. Suddenly she remembered. One of Robert's relatives, no doubt—akin to the old Earl of Wolver. Hadn't there been a Dolph? She had remembered it from her first hearing of it, because the name was strange to her. She had never known either of the boys until she met Robert in London, but it was possible he might know her name, and the scandal that had, at least at the time, been attached to it.

And here the young man was, smiling as he was presented to Sophy, bending over Charlotte's hand a little longer than Fenella liked, and bowing to the governess.

Fenella did not think he recognized her name, since Mrs. Pruitt had forgotten it and substituted a garbled version. But she would take care not to encourage any conversation with him. There were too many questions he might ask that she did not wish to answer.

That night she dreamed again of Oakhurst, and Papa—and woke up in the darkness, crying. It was a long time before she fell asleep again.

Life at Chantrey Manor went on without alteration after the visit to the Pruitts. Young Mr. Thorne had called today, as was often his habit, but also as usual, Fenella stayed in the schoolroom with Emma.

Emma, however, allowed her mind to stray to the salon below. "Do you think we will ever go to London?"

"I should think so, sometime."

"I don't think so. Mama talked to my grandfather, and he roared at her."

"He may change his mind someday."

"When?"

"When Charlotte is older, and you have learned your lessons better. Come, Emma, let us see whether you remember your globe."

Obediently Emma stepped to the new globe, purchased because of Fenella's insistence, and twirled it. "London is right here, isn't it? It doesn't seem very far."

"Far enough," said Fenella crisply. "But there's no need to think about London for some time yet. And Mr. Thorne is here for only a short visit, I suspect."

"The earl—Lord Wolver, you know—sent him to Stockton Priory until he gets here."

Since Fenella had been told that Stockton Priory immediately adjoining Chantrey Manor had been vacant of any family members, she had not quite realized until now to whom the large estate belonged.

"The earl?" was her first exclamation, followed by the thought: but the earl never travels! How can he be coming?

He had never even seen Fenella, unless it was when she was an infant, and surely he would not recognize her now. Nor would he notice a governess, even one with the evocative name of Standish.

Just the same, this was a voice from the past that she wished she had not heard.

At any rate, she thought comfortably, he will be gone soon, and the Fletchers will not be going to London until Sir Eustace decrees the move. She did not think that was likely to happen very soon.

Sir Eustace was a vast grumbling kind of man, dissatisfied with his family, the loss of his only son and heir nagging at him like an aching tooth, for all it had been five years before.

He had no sympathy or apparent liking for his granddaughters, and his tolerance of his daughter-in-law seemed to be based entirely upon the level of comfort she provided to surround him.

Sir Eustace had every reason to think that the state of affairs at Chantrey Manor would continue indefinitely. If others were dissatisfied, they would do well not to trouble him with their complaints. To say truth, he saw no need for anyone to complain. He had hired an excellent cook and did not begrudge anyone a full stomach. He did not stint on wood for the fires, good candles, nor did he ask awkward questions of his daughter-in-law, as to where her pin money had gone.

He was generous in these matters, for he saw no need to add to the considerable fortunes eventually to be put into the hands of his granddaughters, preferring to spend any excess funds on himself.

That singular morning in October, however, after Fenella had been in residence for almost a year, Sir Eustace was to be disillusioned. Change was on its way.

It was the custom at Chantrey Manor to have an early breakfast, early, that is, as compared to what was usual in urban society. Sir Eustace took an active and knowledge-able part in supervising his farms, and was out on his lands at an early hour. This morning had been no exception.

However, a question posed by the farm manager had arisen, and Sir Eustace must return to the house to find the answer. Thus it was that he arrived while the other members of his household were having their breakfast.

Shipley had taken the mail from the footman and brought it in to Sophy, and she had just exclaimed to Charlotte and Fenella, "At last! I knew she would answer my request!"

The excitement on her face faded swiftly as she heard a voice that, at this moment, was the last she wished to hear.

"Who would answer?" asked Sir Eustace, nettled that even the smallest item of household business had not been explained to him.

"I th-thought you were out on the farms," stammered Sophy.

"Well, I'm not. I asked you, who?"

Sophy gathered herself together. "Well, you will have to know sometime."

"I have to know right now."

"It's . . . well, it's a letter from the countess."

"What countess?" demanded Sir Eustace, vaguely alarmed.

Sophy had planned to choose the time and circumstances of telling him, but he had come upon her before she had fabricated appropriate details. Now there was nothing left but to blurt out the truth.

"I wrote to her, that's all. I should think I could write to

my children's great-aunt, after all. Who else,'' she cried,
goaded by his ominous frown into tactless accusations,
"would agree that it is time for my daughter to be married?
Certainly not you, Sir Eustace! How can she ever meet
suitable men locked away in this end of the world?''

"Mama . . ." Charlotte began.

"*Whom* did you say you wrote to?"

Sophy quickly and obviously girded herself for battle.
Voice trembling, but soft brown eyes holding unexpected
steel, she said, "Your sister. The Countess of Crewe."

"Good God, I know my own sister's name. But that name
is not to be mentioned in this house, and you know it!''

"Well, it is very difficult," said Sophy with an air of
reasonableness, "not to inform you of her invitation without
mentioning her name."

Sir Eustace, usually fluent in accusation and invective, was
for this astonishing moment without voice. Fenella,
fascinated as though watching fireworks on Guy Fawkes
Day, heard the astonishing scheme unfold.

Now that Charlotte was eighteen, and Sir Eustace had
given no sign of taking them all to London for the Season,
Sophy had gone behind his back and written to his sister,
a gracious and very social hostess in London, to whom Sir
Eustace had not spoken in ten years.

The countess had responded, inviting Sophy and her girls
to come to London at once.

"Only to spite me!" roared Sir Eustace. "She knows what
would anger me. Interfering again, she is, and I tell you I
won't have it."

"Very well," said Sophy calmly. "I shall have to write
and tell her so. But I imagine that if you yourself do not take
Charlotte to London for her Season, Lady Crewe might find
your conduct something to wonder at. And tell her friends
about, of course."

Goaded beyond endurance, Sir Eustace, roaring as he
went, left the salon and retreated to his upstairs study.

"Well, at least," said Sophy, beginning to tremble now
that the scene was played out, "he didn't say no."

Fenella had thought that Sir Eustace's refusal was as

definite as anyone could expect, but Sophy knew her tyrant better than expected.

The subject came up again later. Sophy had spoken of her own Season in London as a pattern of delights to come.

"Mama, I don't want—" Prudently, Charlotte fell silent.

However, Emma was under no such constraint. "She doesn't want to go to London, not while Mr. Thorne is at the Priory."

"Thorne? You mean the new earl," corrected Sir Eustace. "Is he coming?"

Sophy was easily diverted. "No, she means young Mr. Thorne. The earl's cousin."

Her father-in-law snorted. "No one could be interested in that makeweight! Eyes too close together!"

Fenella found her voice. "The *new* earl, did you say? Did old Lord Wolver die, then?"

Sir Eustace glowered. "Of course he did, or there'd be no new one."

"I hadn't heard."

He continued to berate Sophy, while Fenella's mind scurried among the genealogical miscellany in her mind. Old Lord Wolver had had two grandsons, but the older one had died. Of course, there was still Gervase—he must be the new earl. She knew Gervase well enough so that whenever he might come to visit Stockton Priory she must avoid him, unless—she recalled Lady Warthog in Taunton—unless he refused to recognize her.

Since she had managed to avoid Dolph Thorne at Chantrey Manor, there would likely be no need to face the new Earl of Wolver. Nonetheless, she had not thought that the rush of memory brought on only by the name of a former neighbor —whom she scarcely knew—would bring her such pain.

"Sir Eustace, my daughter is going to London," said Sophy with unaccustomed firmness. "Lady Crewe is expecting us."

"Expect and be damned!" shouted Sir Eustace, heedless of small shuffling sounds in the hall indicating the gathering of servants offstage to enjoy the exciting spectacle.

Sophy, however, appeared unmoved. "I shall discuss this
with you when you are calmer," she told her father-in-law.
For an instant Fenella's mind brought her the picture of a
tigress snarling defiance to protect her cubs. Then the picture
faded, and Sophy seemed her own submissive self again.

But if Sophy seemed unmoved, this was not the case with
Charlotte.

"Mama, I won't! I can't! You should have asked me!"

The last words were indistinct, filtered through a throat
thick with tears. Charlotte leapt to her feet, shoved the chair
back, and rushed headlong from the breakfast room.

"Good God, Sophy!" roared Sir Eustace. "Is this the kind
of decorum you put up with? No better-behaved than a silly
kitchen maid! I won't have it, I tell you!"

Sophy appeared calm, although Fenella noticed her hand
was shaking. "Then you will be so much easier here if we
all go away to London, you see."

Sir Eustace snorted prodigiously, and snarled something,
probably a curse, under his breath before he too stamped
from the room.

It was easy, thought Fenella, to see from whom Charlotte
inherited her uncertain temper.

Sophy smiled kindly upon Fenella. "Do not be concerned
over our small domestic disagreements."

"Disagreements!" The exclamation was forced from
Fenella.

"Well, perhaps more than that," agreed Sophy. "But he'll
come around." She smiled in sly triumph. "I've already
spoken to Miss Tyson, our seamstress, you know, to engage
her time. We shall all need new gowns. I expect you would
wish at least a new walking gown. I shall speak to Miss Tyson
for you."

Sophy clearly had another card or two yet to play, thought
Fenella. For the first time, she looked at Sophy with something akin to respect. She had revealed a startling flair for
intrigue. But however strongly Sophy felt she could persuade
Sir Eustace to allow them their London sojourn, she had less
influence with her daughter. Charlotte refused even to

consider the question, and she was adamant about refusing to coax her grandfather into allowing the trip.

"He never listens to me anyway," Charlotte pointed out. "Why should he now? Besides, I don't want to go to London. All my friends are here."

"The point is," said her mother, "you need to make new friends. I know Mr. Thorne is amusing, but I assure you there are others of equal address in London."

Her words fell on deaf ears. Charlotte would not even go to Miss Tyson to choose new gowns.

It took only a sennight to reveal Sophy's strategy— her determination to take Charlotte to London, to see her well-married, and perhaps, if truth were told, to enjoy herself the parties, routs, drums, excursions, picnics, balls, and flirtations that were usually the lot of any lady in society.

Charlotte had so far resisted all beguilements. In fact, Fenella saw very little of her. She had been told that both girls were heiresses to a considerable fortune from an ancient relative on Sophy's side of the family. Charlotte was an attractive young miss, with the sparkling dark eyes and curly black hair that should certainly bring her to the notice of various gallants in London.

But Charlotte was not in the least enchanted by the prospect of a London Season. Fenella remembered her own excitement when she was introduced into the London social whirl. She had had two halcyon years, culminating in the happy hours when Robert had been at her side.

She shook herself mentally. It did no good to look back. That life was past, gone forever. Papa and Oakhurst were no more, and Robert was not worth a tear.

Although the London visit seemed to be out of the question, Sophy had not yet exhausted her resources. Charlotte might prove difficult to entice into the web. "She is merely shy," Sophy said comfortably. "She must conquer her fear of meeting new people. That is why I wrote to Lady Crewe at the first."

This day Fenella had finished her morning in the school-room, and Emma had been set free for the day. Sophy liked to have Fenella with her, finding her a satisfactory sounding board for her own opinions. Miss Standish never disapproved, never suggested that Sophy might not be correct in her opinions.

Even so, Fenella found it hard at this moment to keep her own counsel. She had not noticed Charlotte's shyness. Indeed, she would have thought the girl overly outgoing for a well-brought-up daughter of a respected family. Sophy considered her as having merely a friendly disposition. As friendly as a puppy, Fenella considered, and as unfit for London society.

Sir Eustace controlled the money, both Sophy's and the fortunes of his granddaughters. And he was adamant in his refusal to allow them to go to London.

Until, that is, his comfort was challenged, as it came to be.

Another letter arrived from Lady Crewe, but this time addressed to him. He had long since severed any sibling relationship, since the Earl of Crewe had called him an assortment of uncomplimentary epithets. His sister had sided with her husband, and the rift had been complete and satisfactory to both sides. To receive a letter from Alice, Countess of Crewe, then, was an event so unexpected as to be highly suspicious. Indeed, the meat of it was not to Sir Eustace's liking.

Sending for Fenella, he said, "Girls going along all right? Learning well? Behaving themselves?" Without waiting for an answer, he continued, "Well, then, here's news for you. You're going to London!"

"I am?"

"Sophy's bent on going. I don't like it much, but then . . . women! But you will have the spending of the money. I don't trust any one of them with a farthing. But I'll put the money in your hands. That'll hold them in!"

Fenella did not wish to go, nor did she relish the prospect of telling Sophy that she had spent her limit of money. She dreaded to meet Robert again, even by chance. She might see many of her former acquaintances—and be snubbed again. But her arguments, which of course contained nothing of her real reasons for avoiding London, availed her nothing.

Not until she rose to go, and looked meaningfully at the missive on the surface of the desk, did she begin to understand Sir Eustace's change of heart.

She recognized the handwriting as identical to that of Lady Crewe's note to Sophy, which had been thrust at Fenella to read.

Involuntarily, she exclaimed, "From Lady Crewe?" Immediately she bit her lip. Sir Eustace's correspondence was none of her affair.

But Sir Eustace was not offended. Sheepishly he gestured at the letter. "From my sister. Says if Sophy and the girls don't go to London, she'll come down to Chantrey Manor—for a long stay with me. She'll do that over my corpse, I'll tell you that!"

7

At this moment, however, London seemed removed to a great distance.

The schoolroom on the third floor of Chantrey Manor was, as always, pleasantly warm. A bright fire burned in the grate, and a stray sunbeam slanted through the windows at an angle which promised that spring was on the rise.

The inhabitants of the schoolroom were in their diverse ways indulging thoughts far removed from the irregular French verbs that were the topic of this hour's study. The student—"Must I always say *élève*, Miss Standish? I don't feel like an ee-leve."

"Nor," said Fenella, slightly amused, "is your pronunciation in the least like one. I should not call you a student at all, Emma." Then, in an altered tone, she cried, "Muggins! What on earth are you doing?"

The third inhabitant of the room, answering frequently but not always to the name Muggins, was a small dog of no distinction but immense loyalty, centered on Fenella. He had appeared at the kitchen door one morning, a stray from no one knew where. Cook would have chased him away with a mop, had Fenella not been at hand to salvage him. Just now he favored her with an appealing look of innocence, somewhat spoiled by the crumbs of breakfast biscuit clinging to his nose.

"I saved that to eat later, you naughty dog!" But the tone in which Fenella spoke was too gentle to raise the slightest objection in the animal's mind, and he bent to finish off his lucky find.

Fenella, with an exasperated but affectionate look at the dog, took up the tools of her trade once more. "Emma . . ."

But Emma had gone to the window, and something in the set of her shoulders aroused a sense of uneasiness in Fenella. She liked Emma much better than she had any of the Hervey children, and thought that she might eventually become resigned to her swift descent from being Miss Fenella Standish of Oakhurst, only child of a doting father and betrothed happily to a man whose name she could not even yet say without resentment, to being an orphan, without funds, and of course without a fiancé.

In the nearly twelve months she had been at Chantrey Manor, Fenella had found the eighteen-year-old Charlotte sadly uninterested in the usages of polite society. However, by this time Fenella had grown fond of her young charge, and now she joined her at the window.

From the advantage of the third floor, Fenella could see far down the valley. The river wound through broad fields on its way to the sea, some distance away. The gently sloping hillsides were covered with great trees, possibly part of the original forest that once covered the island.

Far across the faint spring green of the treetops, rising like a white finger pointing to the sky, was the tower of Stockton Priory, nearest neighbor to Chantrey Manor. The owner, whom she knew now had been her old neighbor Lord Wolver, had visited this manor only infrequently during his reclusive life. And the new earl had not yet come to inspect his new property.

The only interest it held for Fenella, and a very mild interest at that, was that it was the current residence of Dolph Thorne.

Although the tower looked near enough to toss a stone at, by the road it was nearly a five-mile drive away. Idly Fenella saw far down the valley a plume of dust rising slowly into the quiet air. The countryside was still dry, still dusty, still in urgent need of the spring rains which again this year were late.

"Come on, Emma," she urged at last. "Back to *vivre* and the rest, like a good *élève*."

Slowly Emma returned to her chair. "But why do I have to learn French at all?"

"Because your mother wishes it, because your grandfather wishes it, and because you will find it most useful."

"But our army will beat Napoleon, won't they? So won't they all speak English then?"

Fenella laughed. "Well, now, you remember we heard from Squire Clavering that the Tzar of Russia has joined with the duke's armies and the King of Prussia as well. So why shouldn't the French then be speaking Russian?"

"Because English is easier," said Emma triumphantly.

"You will wish," said Fenella, trying to regain her proper governess frame of mind, "to give the impression that you are a well-brought-up, well-educated young lady. And all young ladies in London speak fluent French."

Emma's shrewd glance suggested that she did not believe this any more than Fenella did, but she did not challenge her. "Did you have a Season?"

"Yes, of course."

"But I thought—"

Swiftly Fenella interrupted. "You thought that governesses did not have Seasons. You are right. But you know I was not a governess in my cradle. In fact, I was simply frittering away my time—"

"Frittering?"

"As I said—until my fairy godmother told me that Emma Fletcher would need someone to help her with her French verbs, and here I am."

Nonsense like this frequently brought Emma—not possessed of a powerful intellect—to a fit of giggles, following which Fenella could bring her back to her books. But the strategy did not succeed this time.

Emma was still troubled. "But a married lady would not be going to London for the Season, would she? Isn't that the reason why everybody goes? To get married?"

"You are too wise," said Fenella with a little laugh.

"Charlotte will make a fine match this spring, and then,

when she is married, it will be your turn.'' Emma did not answer. ''And now,'' said Fenella, determinedly cheerful, ''you'll all be going to London very soon, and you won't know your verbs. But perhaps you can pretend a speech impediment—nothing serious, of course, but one that discommodes you until you can catch up. You'll be coming out yourself in a few years, you know.''

''I'll never get to London, not this time,'' wailed Emma, suddenly disconsolate, ''and I'll forget all my French by then anyway.''

Forgetting all her French would be for Emma the work of a day, thought Fenella, aware of the extent of the child's learning. ''But surely your mama will not leave you behind?''

When Sophy learned that Sir Eustace intended to place Fenella in charge of the funds, Fenella might well be out of a position when Sophy and her girls left for London. Besides, Fenella had no desire to see London again, burdened as she was with a trunkload of memories.

No—Fenella was not anxious to see London again, where Papa had danced the first dance with her at her very first party, and where Robert had . . .

She would be sorry to see this post finished, not only because she knew how hard it would be to obtain another one. She was well-regarded here, even though Sophy managed to move many of the burdens of housekeeping onto Fenella's shoulders.

But Emma had been speaking—while, as in a dream, Fenella, in a frothy white gown, her hair dressed and ornamented with pearls, had once again in fancy curtsied before the Regent and felt his fat fingers chucking her kindly under the chin—and now Fenella came back to reality with a thud.

''Dolph is old, isn't he?''

''Dolph?'' echoed Fenella vaguely. Then she remembered. ''You mean Mr. Thorne?''

''Charlotte calls him Dolph. She sees him all the time, you know.''

''I didn't know,'' said Fenella. ''But what does his age

matter? If your mother receives him, it is only a social duty, after all.''

''He *is* old, isn't he?'' Emma persisted.

Fenella brought him clearly to her mind. Old? She hadn't considered the question. She had seen him only once, but she recalled his sandy features, which would not show the slightest age even twenty years fromnow, and his blond hair, which would turn unobtrusively gray when the time came.

''I would imagine he might be twenty-five.''

''I don't like him.''

''Now, Emma, there is no need to like him. He is related to the new earl, a distant cousin, as I recall, and you must be civil to him. But why the interest? Simply to avoid studying?''

''Charlotte meets him.''

''Of course she does. When he comes to call, it is most proper that your mama should send for her. After all, she is out of the schoolroom.''

''I don't like him. He does funny things.''

''Don't gossip, Emma.''

Emma sat down with a sigh. How queer adults were! If you tried to tell them something, they said, ''Don't gossip.'' But if you knew something and didn't tell them, they screamed, ''Why didn't you?'' Resigned, Emma picked up her book again, and began to recite.

Not until Floss came up, her housemaid's cap awry, carrying a tray of small cakes to tide scholar and teacher over until luncheon, did Emma return to the subject, and then it was not of her own doing, but her maid's.

''Miss Charlotte isn't here, then?''

''No, she isn't.''

Floss peered nearsightedly around the room, as though Emma had tucked her sister away under the bed. ''Then where . . . ?''

Something in her nervous manner struck Fenella. ''Isn't she in her room? Or with her mother?''

Or in one or another of the likely places? Fenella finally

mentioned the rose arbor, simply because she could think of no more possible places for a daughter of the house to be.

After Floss left, saying that she hadn't thought of that, Fenella's eyes fell on her pupil. She should have recognized it before, she thought with an inner sigh. Emma had that air of suppressed excitement which in her often heralded an unpleasant but trivial incident, usually some dereliction of the servants.

But this time there was a hint of something else that Fenella could not identify, and with a sinking heart she suspected that she should have probed more deeply an hour or so since.

"Now, Emma," she said after Floss was gone, "I think you have something to tell me."

Now that the way was clear, Emma turned mutinous. After a few moments of silence, Fenella set herself to extract whatever there was to hear.

"You say," said Fenella, casting back in her memory, "that you are not going to London?"

"Not just me. Nobody's going."

If that decision had been made, Fenella had not heard of it. "How do you know this?"

"You said."

"Now, Emma," warned Fenella.

"Well, but you did say that a married lady would not be going. That is, would not *need* to be going."

"Well, I suppose I implied that. But surely you are not speaking of your mother!" Who had been, but was no longer, a married lady.

"No. I mean Charlotte."

Fenella's astonishment was held in check with some difficulty. She finally said, with commendable control, "Emma, I think you must tell me what you are talking about."

Thus adjured, and coaxed sufficiently to soothe her wounded feelings, Emma complied. "Well, Charlotte isn't precisely married."

Fenella breathed more easily. Emma had doubtless discovered a mare's nest, and would glory in being the center of attention—

"But she will be by tonight," said Emma, "or maybe tomorrow."

"Tomorrow?" echoed Fenella faintly.

"I suppose so. It doesn't take very long to get to that place in Scotland, does it?"

"Gretna Green," confirmed Fenella. Then, as the full enormity of the situation burst on her, she cried, "Emma!"

And at last, convinced of the gravity of the secret she had been carrying, Emma explained.

Charlotte had been meeting Dolph Thorne secretly, and today she was running away with him.

"She couldn't!" cried Fenella, outraged.

"But she took her clothes," Emma pointed out.

Fenella hurried down to the next floor below, followed by Emma, full of excitement, and Muggins, mystified but ever loyal.

Fenella searched Charlotte's closets. Gone were her driving suit, the new hat with the fetching plume, two morning gowns of muslin, and a braid-trimmed afternoon dress.

"And your bandbox, Miss Standish," Emma said helpfully.

"But . . . but why?"

"Dolph says," Emma said, scorn edging her voice, "that he's not letting his little Charlotte get away from him all the way to London. Little! She's two inches taller than I am!"

Fenella shot her a swift glance. Eavesdropping again, obviously. At this point Fenella could not chide the girl. If what she had overheard was true, then the situation was enormously serious.

Fenella hurried down the hall from Charlotte's room to her mother's suite, overlooking the west lawn, Emma close behind.

"Mama's gone over to Mrs. Pruitt's. Took the carriage, too."

"And Sir Eustace will be out on the farm somewhere. How long ago did they go? But you don't know, do you?"

"A while ago. Dolph was waiting for her in the woods.

In a phaeton, he calls it. Are we going after them? All the way to Scotland?''

There was nothing else to do. Surely they would not set off for the border in a phaeton. For one thing, where would they put the bandbox?

If they had not got much of a start, then perhaps she could catch up with them. If Sophy had the carriage, then the curricle must still be available, if Emma was right about the phaeton. And surely Charlotte could not have taken the curricle, for the grooms would certainly have noticed the bandbox, and she would not have been allowed to leave.

Emma followed Fenella, now carrying a shawl and wearing a round bonnet, to the stables. Unnoticed by either, Muggins was following, fully aware that something was afoot, and whatever that something was, it could mean a ride in the curricle, the pinnacle of his canine heart's desire.

''I am going after them,'' said Fenella at last, ''but you must stay here and inform Sir Eustace or your mother where I have gone. And why. Now, back to the house, lest the groom become curious.''

Under Fenella's steady eye, Emma moved reluctantly back to the house.

''I'll go alone,'' Fenella told Beccles as she mounted into the curricle. Standing beside the groom was Muggins, the long-haired gray dog, his wistful gaze on her so appealing that she hesitated. Muggins was no mastiff, but he was better than no help at all, and his shrill bark with a shivering tremolo at the end might serve as a weapon of surprise, in case of need.

''Come on, then,'' said Fenella. The little dog was beside her before she finished the words. ''You'll be someone to talk to.''

''Sure you can handle the reins, miss?'' asked the groom doubtfully, still not convinced he was to stay behind.

For answer, she backed the curricle neatly, swung it around in a tight circle, and set off down the drive, scattering gravel.

Papa had had no idea that his beloved daughter would ever

use the skill he taught her in mounting a single-handed chase after a foolish miss already, no doubt, on her way to Gretna Green with a man who must be reckless in the extreme to take advantage of her.

She knew that the groom thought it excessively odd, if not downright improper, for her to go tearing off alone, without even a stableboy for company, but the fewer servants who knew about Charlotte's disgrace—supposing Fenella to arrive too late—the better.

Even if she managed to reach Stockton Priory—surely the first place to look for them—in time, Charlotte was not one to see the value of discretion. They would be fortunate indeed to get out of this scrape without scandal, to say naught of credit.

"Well," said Fenella to Muggins, "she's not my charge, after all. Her grandfather can deal with her when I get her back." After a moment she added, "*If* I get her back."

8

Stockton Priory had stood empty for all the years of the earl's invalidism—empty, that is, save for a small house staff of butler, cook, footmen, head groom (but with only one assistant), one stableboy, three housemaids, and two gardeners.

None of this, of course, did Fenella know. In truth she was not even certain as to the road leading to the Priory itself, but she had a good sense of direction, and she felt sure of finding the house eventually.

If haste had not been of the utmost importance on this occasion, she would have enjoyed the drive. Not for three years had she gone driving in her own curricle, alone save for an escort. At home her escort would have been at the least an assistant groom. Here, a world away, she was accompanied only by a furry four-legged creature of immense goodwill.

"And of the alternatives," she told Muggins, "I find you the more charming companion."

The little dog gave a snort, quite agreeing with her.

After some miles, she slowed and began to examine the road with interest. She was well on the way to Shackleton, the small village in the valley where most of the purchases for Chantrey Manor were made.

"I know that Stockton Priory is not on this road, Muggins, but it is surely closer to Shackleton than Chantrey, is it not? What did Emma say—Dolph was waiting for Charlotte in the forest? Probably the woods along the boundary of Chantrey. The little idiot! Her head is stuffed full of romantic nonsense, and I wish I knew where she obtained such reading material!''

She thought a moment, reviewing her knowledge of the road ahead. "Certainly," she said at last, "there must be a road just along here."

She brought the horse to a halt. Ahead of her a few yards stood the great oak, old beyond counting, half-dead from lightning strikes over its long years. The tree marked the edge of the higher ground. Beyond the tree the slope dropped sharply into the wide valley.

She knew the road well from this point on. Midway down the valley, as she watched, a scattered cloud of sand-colored dust rose in the still air. Someone was traveling fast, and likely not in a farm cart, either!

Suddenly she felt a chill. Was that vehicle carrying the runaways? When she ascertained that this traveler was coming in her direction, although at least a couple of miles away, she breathed again. There was still a chance that she was in good time to prevent Charlotte's folly from becoming disaster.

"Now, Muggins, let's find that road."

The drive to the Priory wound through the home woods for what seemed an unnecessarily long distance. This manor was only one of the holdings of the wealthy Earl of Wolver, and a minor one at that, yet the length of the drive indicated substantial acreage.

At length, she made one last turn. The drive debouched on the extensive parkland surrounding the house itself.

The Priory was an imposing building. At the center of the facade stood a tower of white stone, probably part of the original religious structure. The tower, built well before the time of Henry VIII, had been added to in both directions, and no doubt also at the back, so that if monks still walked in the haunts of the Priory they would find very little of their original home. Even the carp ponds had doubtless been filled in centuries before.

However, Fenella's business was not with monks. Going, as it were, from the ancient sublime of the Priory, her gaze fell on the courtyard behind the great house, and the scene that met her eyes bordered on the ridiculous!

She had not come in pursuit of Charlotte in vain. And she had come in time.

In the center of the courtyard, dwarfing the servants scuttling around it, stood a great traveling chariot. Fenella, bemused, still sat in her curricle, holding the reins. Her grandmother had traveled to Bath in one such vehicle, followed by wagons full of servants, bedding, plate, and other comforts. Surely this vehicle before her had not had cattle between its shafts since the time of the old countess, dead before Fenella was born.

With one hand she gentled Muggins, who took notable exception to the scene before him, growling fiercely. The persons dealing with the chariot were transfixed with surprise at her appearance.

They ceased immediately their labors of tying an unwieldy trunk onto the roof of the chariot, and shrill cries of instruction from Charlotte failed to move them. Fenella thought she detected a certain relief in their withdrawal to await events. They certainly knew that the enterprise they were compelled to abet was not up to snuff.

Off to one side of the stableyard stood a team of less-than-prime cattle, eyeing without equine enthusiasm the vast unwieldly carriage that they knew would be theirs to pull.

Various items of baggage, some of which Fenella knew came from Chantrey Manor, stood on the ground ready to be packed in the interior of the coach. Indeed, Fenella recognized one of them as her own bandbox.

From behind the chariot appeared Dolph Thorne, a harried man. "Hurry up, Flint!" he cried to the head groom. "There's no time to lose!"

Flint gave him a scathing look. Clearly he had no great opinion of young Mr. Thorne. Sending a stableboy to hold Fenella's horses, he himself went to help the visiting young lady down from the curricle. There was such an obvious expression of disgust on his face that she guessed rightly that the servants, not approving of any such doubtful enterprise, had by their deliberate delays upset the schedule of the elopement.

Muggins had by this time discovered there were other canines present, and hurled defiance at them. Fenella plucked him off the seat and held him, but he continued to bark.

She stepped briskly into the midst of the assembly. Charlotte watched her approach. She was clearly in the throes, not of shame, but of disappointment. Dolph Thorne wore an expression of resignation, as though, knowing her arrival meant the dashing of his hopes, nothing were left to him.

Fenella judged it best to move directly to the attack.

"Charlotte, I do not recall giving permission for you to use my luggage."

"Oh, Fenella! Why did you have to come at this very moment? In another half-hour we would be gone!"

"That is precisely why I came, young lady. I cannot believe that you are so lost to propriety as to travel *anywhere* with a gentleman, even in a tilbury. But a great closed chariot like this? Outrageous! Of course I must be mistaken about your intentions."

"You're not my mother!" Charlotte blazed, her face flushed and her prominent eyes bulging.

"Quite right, and I thank God for it. Charlotte, I do not scruple to tell you that I have no interest in your plans, as hen-witted as they are. However, I do admit to some curiosity as to the destination of my bandbox."

Under his breath Flint muttered, "Gretna Green for certain, miss."

"You have no right to interfere, Miss . . ." interrupted Dolph without heat. She suspected that, with premature discovery, he had lost his taste for this business.

"Of course I don't," said Fenella bracingly, "and you are quite right to tell me your actions are none of my affair. But Miss Fletcher is my concern. I suggest you give some thought to this, Charlotte. You know you will be ruined if you continue this idiotic escapade."

"No, I won't!"

As though she had not spoken, Fenella added, "I've come to bring you home."

"I shall not go! Dolph, tell her to go away!"

Dolph did not move. It was clear to Fenella then that her suspicions were justified—that with her own arrival at the scene, some of the joyous spontaneity had gone out of the day for Dolph Thorne. She noticed that his glance fell often upon the opening of the drive, as though he were expecting someone else. Probably he was anxious lest Sir Eustace arrive in full cry.

"You can't stop us!" cried Charlotte. "We'll run you over, see if we won't! Flint, get the horses ready!"

"Now," said Fenella, losing her patience at last, "that is outside of enough! While I do not intend to throw the curricle across your path—I do have more compassion for the poor horses than I have for you, you know—as soon as I inform Sir Eustace that you have started on your journey to the border, you may be sure that the hue and cry will be raised." She paused to think. "I wonder whether they still follow that custom? It will be interesting to see."

Mr. Thorne, seeing that she was determined to stop their flight, took a different tack. "We cannot persuade you to silence?"

"Not," said Fenella pleasantly, "unless you intend to throw me into the earl's cellars."

For a timeless second she saw something ugly flicker in the back of his eyes. For that tiny moment she felt a coldness creep over her. She wished she had not even mentioned the earl's cellars. This man could be, she was suddenly convinced, capable of unpleasant violence. He was sorely tempted to follow her suggestion, she thought, but with Flint and, by this time, a large man addressed as Napier, who was obviously the butler, and two muscular footmen at the scene as unfriendly witnesses, Dolph wavered.

Seeing she had won, she turned to Flint and said, "Do you think you could secure Miss Fletcher's luggage on the back of the curricle?"

Dolph's lips tightened and he glared as the servants sprang with alacrity to untie trunks from the roof and sort out the smaller valises and bandboxes on the ground.

"Not the trunk, miss," said Flint. "We can send it this afternoon." He thought a moment, then added tactfully, "We can take the road through the woods to the stable, if that would suit?"

"Eminently," said Fenella. "Now, Charlotte, pray get into the curricle. Your mother will be anxious about your absence."

"She need not," exploded Charlotte. "I told her I would not go to London, not while Dolph is here. We are going to be married, and no one can stop us!"

She stood mutinously beside Dolph, nibbling at her thumb. Made conscious by Fenella's amused glance that her habit was a mark of her childishness, she pulled her hand away at once.

Dolph said, his voice rough, "All right, Charlotte. We're going this minute, in spite of this interfering governess, or we're not going at all."

"Oh, Dolph!" she cried, throwing her arms around him. "Don't say that! We have to go!"

"To Gretna Green?" murmured Fenella. "Now, what can be the cause of such urgency?"

Am I already too late? Have things gone farther with these two than . . . ? She could not believe it of a delicately nurtured girl, even though she had no more sense than a goose.

But even more convincingly, she did not believe that Dolph Thorne would so far forget himself as to seduce—elope and marry, yes, seduce, no—a girl of good family.

Charlotte was torn now between retreating to the chariot with Dolph and regaining possession of the bandbox now roped to the curricle.

Fenella's hearing was more acute than that of most persons, and she was the first to catch the sound of wheels on the driveway and the steady, slow pounding of horses' hooves.

Later Fenella tried to imagine the scene that must have presented itself to the new arrival as the incoming equipage emerged from the woods.

Charlotte clutched Dolph's sleeve, until he shook her off and groaned, "It's too late!"

Fenella's curricle stood, luggage roped to the boot. She turned an expectant glance toward the newcomer. Muggins, finding recent developments puzzling, had fallen silent.

All of the participants seemed to be struck into immobility as the carriage came into full view and moved in stately fashion toward the gate to the stableyard.

The vehicle was black, the wheels pricked out in yellow, glossy even though covered with a film of road dust. The cattle were of an appearance so superior to those standing mutely harnessed in the yard ready for the ancient chariot as to seem a different breed altogether.

Dolph said under his breath, "Why could he not have waited one more day?"

A liveried groom dropped to the ground and set the steps at the carriage door, and the new Earl of Wolver descended to stand, at last, on this portion of his own land.

Fenella watched, transfixed, as he came toward them.

She had not dreamed for some months, but the dream returned in such force as to seem as real as Muggins in her arms. Again she had that peculiar clutch in her breast, that sense of being unable to draw breath. A dream only—it had to be!

Robert Thorne could not possibly be standing no more than ten feet away from her.

She opened her lips to speak . . .

But when he turned deliberately toward her, his glance passed over her as though she were a mere figure in the background of an unedifying pantomime.

With something akin to despair, she realized with force that she was not merely a servant. She had refused his offer of marriage, thinking herself unworthy because undowered, and he had done nothing to disabuse her mind of that conviction. Now, titled and wealthy, he was immeasurably above her present station.

She could now see the measure of her great folly!

9

The new Lord Wolver, although preserving utter calm, had received a severe blow. This lady bore a most uncanny resemblance to the lady whom he had once hoped to marry, but this lady—some kind of servant, by her dress—was more slender, somehow more mature than Fenella. He had lost his lady, to his vast regret even yet. But was he now to see her face in every woman he met?

At this moment, the scene before him in its entirety must be dealt with. Standing at his ease, he nodded coolly in Fenella's direction. It was clear to her, however, that he was taking notice of Charlotte, who now stood beside her. He seemed unaware of the flush that burned Fenella's cheeks, and instead focused a penetrating blue gaze on his cousin Dolph.

Fenella believed he had dismissed her as though she barely existed, or as though her intelligence were insufficient to furnish any kind of acceptable explanation of this very odd tableau in his stableyard.

Far from any sentiment of gratitude to him for respecting her privacy, her feeling at the moment was one of rising anger tending toward the explosive. How dared he treat her like . . . like a servant?

She could understand Lady Warthog's snubbing her on the street—after all, Fenella had lost entirely her firm footing on the social ladder. But not the man who had wished her to share his future.

She closed her eyes, lest Lord Wolver see the pain that

seized her totally unexpectedly. When she opened them
again, nothing had changed. A lifetime had been lived in that
moment, she thought ruefully, and yet Lord Wolver stood
quietly, self-possessed, engaged in pulling his gloves off, and
regarding his cousin without favor.

"Rudolph?" said Lord Wolver.

"Well, Lord Wolver?" said Dolph with a sneer.

"I confess I am surprised to see you here at Stockton
Priory," said its owner. "I had thought you out of the
country. Why do I think of Ireland?"

"Perhaps," said Dolph with returning confidence, seeing
that his cousin had not ripped up at him at the start, "because
I am frequently there. But I made sure you would extend
me every hospitality, *cousin,* now that you have succeeded
to the old man's title."

"Perhaps I should have, had you requested it. As it
is . . ."

Lord Wolver—it helped Fenella to think of him in that style
rather than by the more intimate *Robert*—turned then to
Fenella. For one kindling moment, something flickered in
his eyes. She knew he recognized her then. But the next
moment she saw only indifference in his gaze.

Suddenly she was aware of the figure she must cut. She
had not paid attention to her attire before she rode out from
the Manor, since she was persuaded that haste was essential
in order to rescue Charlotte before she had actually left for
Gretna Green. She had tied on a bonnet, true, but it had,
with the breeze engendered by her fast driving, fallen
lopsided over her right ear. She had come in her morning
muslin, and she was sure that Muggins had bestowed his hair
generously on her sleeves.

She looked ready to sweep out the kitchen, she thought.
But then, what difference would it make were she dressed
in rose brocade, her hair twisted in the latest fashion, a gauzy
shawl trimmed with silver adjusted with infinite care around
her shoulders? He had seen her thus before, and did not truly
love her then. Only from his compassion for a distressed lady
had sprung his offer.

She caught her own automatic gesture toward straightening

her bonnet. She would not, though she died, give Lord Wolver the impression that she cared any more what he thought of her. He had already given sufficient evidence of what his impression was.

He turned back to his cousin. "I must assume there is an explanation of all this . . . this activity in my stableyard?"

Dolph replied, "Should you not send your carriage down to the stables? I fancy you will not like your cattle to stand. Prime ones they are, too."

Robert looked appreciatively at the chariot. "Our great-aunt's, I assume. I have not seen it since I was a child. I must say you have kept it in excellent condition—is it Flint? Yes, I recall you. It's been some years since I visited here."

"You were but a lad, my lord." The head groom grinned, much gratified.

"Now, why do I suppose that the late countess's carriage is intended to convey a bride and groom to Gretna Green? Surely you know better, Dolph."

Since Lord Wolver's servant, after speaking to the man running to the head of the team as it stopped, had at the start murmured something to his master as the latter approached the tongue-tied little group, Fenella could only suppose that word had passed swiftly as the wind.

Time stretched out endlessly to Fenella. Wouldn't they ever straighten the situation out? They all stood there like a troupe of traveling players who had forgotten their lines. She watched Lord Wolver's carriage move with slow dignity down the slight incline to the stables. The outriders and the groom and his assistant were dismissed by a slight wave of the earl's hand, and only his man lingered, a short distance away.

For the first time, she wondered why this man—one of the collateral Thornes, as she knew—had inherited the title. Obviously the second Sandys son had died on the Peninsula, and so removed from society had she been that she did not know it.

More to stifle the immediate tumult in her thoughts than because she was deliberately shielding Charlotte, Fenella spoke, her tone crisper than she intended. "I am persuaded that very little as a rule will escape your notice, Lord Wolver. You have come at an opportune moment. Rather than attempt to explain to your lordship precisely the situation—"

Lord Wolver gave her his full attention now. Under the impact of those dark blue eyes, her voice faltered. And why should she feel so guilty, as though caught with her hand in the biscuit box?

Lord Wolver's unwavering gaze seemed to bore quite through her. "I agree, ma'am. It would be quite impossible to explain this scene in a way to reflect credit upon any individual."

Her cheeks flushed with anger. She had not forgotten, not really, that she was a Standish. Poor and disgraced, yet she was not a lesser creature than the fashionable Earl of Wolver, and if he did not know it now, she would make sure he did in the future.

Oh, what was she thinking! The earl was nothing to her, nor she to him. She had best go home and practice being a governess!

When the earl had stepped down from his traveling coach, he had given the impression of being monumentally uninterested in the scene that met his eyes. But after that first glance at the elder of the two ladies, he hardly knew what to say. Certainly his thoughts were circling madly. In truth, this shabby elopement engineered by his cousin Dolph had no power to compel his attention now.

In that one moment when his second glance met the indignant eyes of the lady with the bonnet alop, he had been sure of her. She was not an illusion, but a very real and angry woman, and he knew her well.

But how very odd it seemed to find her here in the wild of the North Country, in his own grounds! Moreover, the fashionable beauty he had loved—did he still love her?— was hardly visible in this plainly dressed woman, obviously in a state of agitation somehow connected with his cousin Dolph.

Although he had made some inquiries about her whereabouts after the day she had royally snubbed him three years ago, and had searched for her face in the crowds at every event for the next six months, he had given up any hope of seeing her again.

Now, here she was!

His first impulse was to gather her up in his embrace and shout: Eureka! I have found her again! A glance into those level gray eyes dissuaded him swiftly from such an unconsidered response.

The next moment found him relieved that he had not given way to his impulse. Somewhere in his mind, caution stirred. Fenella, it seemed, had chosen not to recognize him. Therefore, he could not embarrass her with his tactless recollections of the past they shared.

Besides, there was here a situation he did not understand. She was dressed modestly—that bonnet was far from fashionable, with not even a plume to adorn it, even though, cocked as it was over her left eye, he found it charming.

He must sort this out before he could follow his own inclinations. If she were in trouble, then he would deliver her from it. If she were playing a role for whatever reason, he would not queer her pitch.

Nonetheless, the tableau spread before him—his Fenella, manifestly distressed, the schoolroom miss giving every indication of dissolving into strong hysterics, and his malicious cousin Dolph eyeing him in a most challenging manner—would have amused him had he not considered the situation to be grave.

It was time to put an end to it. "Cousin," he said, deliberately allowing his amusement to be evident, "I suspect you have gotten yourself into another scrape, but I do not wish to hear about it at this moment."

"I assure you—" Dolph began, at the same moment as his intended bride broke into impassioned speech.

"You're cruel and unfeeling!" she cried, addressing Lord Wolver. "Dolph said you would blame him for everything! But it's not true! We *are* going to be married, and if we have to go to Gretna Green, then we shall. I've packed my bandbox—"

"*My* bandbox," Fenella said crisply.

"And Mama's going to make me go to London to find a husband, and I don't want one!"

"Then," said Fenella, noting with alarm the girl's rising voice, heralding what could be a very unpleasant scene, "why go to Gretna?"

Charlotte turned on her. "Why do you care? Mama sent you, didn't she? I'd think you'd enough to do with Emma!"

Lord Wolver watched this scene with interest. It became apparent to him that Fenella made up a part of what must be a very odd household. The mention of Emma puzzled him. Could Fenella be a nurse to a patient? Then, remarking the extreme youth of the young miss now engaged in a scene dramatic enough to merit applause at Covent Garden, he suspected that Emma must be a younger sister, still in the schoolroom.

Was Fenella a governess? That surely was the most likely explanation.

More from an urgent wish to stem the tide of recriminations than from prudence, Robert said in a low voice to the lady, "I should not have expected one of your quality to be engaged in any way in such an ill-judged affair as an elopement."

She turned away from Charlotte. Her uplifted face held an expression that stopped him abruptly. Full of indignation, mixed with resentment that he seemed to misunderstand her role here, her gray eyes darkened. At that moment he was more aware of her than he had been—how long ago!—when holding her safe in his arms.

But more than that, he had an indelible impression of extreme hurt, of an animal sorely wounded. He found no words to say.

Unaware of the effect she had on him, she was moved only to respond to the injustice of his remark. "If you had given the slightest heed to what people are saying to you"—she gestured widely, including servants and principals in the drama—"you would realize that Charlotte is very young, scarcely out of the schoolroom, and I suspect she has no idea of what an elopement means. I cannot believe you do not see the unconscionable behavior of that . . . that gentleman! But of course he is your kinsman, and I would expect you to be partial to him.''

Dolph's hearing was acute, and while that conversation was not intended as general, he picked up sufficient of the words as to become avidly interested. To his eyes, his cousin Robert was behaving oddly. Robert should have, if Dolph read him aright, dismissed Charlotte and the governess as though they were a pair of sheep, and then consigned Dolph to a scathing session in the library.

But Robert seemed surprisingly without anger. Perhaps there was something here that could be put to use—Dolph's use, of course.

Fenella continued. ''Your aunt was not the only person who would not approve of Mr. Thorne's behavior,'' she said coldly. ''However, it seems that we have both arrived in time to prevent further damage.''

The tone of her voice informed Muggins that all was not well with his adored lady, and rightly surmising that the enemy was the tall man just opposite, he began to bark in loud indignation.

Fenella paid her champion no heed. She said, raising her voice over the dog's protests, ''I am sure you are too much a gentleman to bruit this incident abroad, especially since your cousin bears such a blameworthy part in it.''

She turned to Charlotte. ''Get up in the curricle, and take the dog.'' She ignored Lord Wolver, who was watching her, fascinated. She handed Muggins to the girl, and grasped her skirt to mount the step herself. She found Lord Wolver at her side, ready to hand her up.

''Do you have all the young lady's luggage?'' he asked.

Startled, Fenella realized that Lord Wolver believed all the trunks to be Charlotte's. ''Your head groom—Flint, I think?—offered to send the one trunk over later. Unless, my lord, you object?''

''My pleasure is to serve your convenience,'' he said with a bow.

All she wanted was to get away, far away from Lord

Wolver and his dark blue eyes and his gallantry, which she perceived as insincere, and the luggage might lie by the wayside for all she cared.

Charlotte by this time had extended her nerves as far as they wished to go. "My bandbox! My new hat with the plume!" she wailed.

"Be quiet!" Fenella ordered, exasperated. "You're upsetting Muggins!"

Fenella's eyes caught the steady gaze of Lord Wolver, and caught the unexpected laughter deep in his eyes. Another time, in her former life, she had often found his amusement contagious, and her anger would then dissipate like bubbles in a breeze. But, increasingly aware of the gulf between them now, not this time.

"Pray stand aside," she ordered him coldly. She picked up the reins from the patient groom, who had been standing at the animal's head throughout the proceedings, and turned the curricle expertly in a tight little circle. Then, without a backward glance, she put the horses quickly into a trot, and soon the shambles of the elopement scene, so rudely interrupted by herself and the earl, was out of sight behind her.

Traveling the length of the driveway, she turned right through the gates of Stockton Priory and retraced the way she had come from Chantrey Manor.

"Don't say a word to me, Charlotte! I am so angry with you! How could you think of eloping to Gretna Green with a young man you scarcely know? Or with anybody, for that matter?"

"I l-love him! And he loves me!"

Fenella allowed herself a small ladylike snort as response.

Love! She knew what love was! She had thought it made up of shared pleasures, of contentment in another's company, of basking in the security of another's regard. But she had also thought it meant loyalty, cleaving together in time of trouble, in reassurance, in understanding—and love had certainly failed her in that sense.

Eventually Charlotte conquered her sobs—which Fenella suspected partook as much of thwarted temper as of desolation—and by the time they reached the gate to the forest lane leading to the stables of Chantrey Manor, the girl had recovered sufficiently to beg Fenella, "I suppose you have to report to my mother."

"Since your mother did not send me after you, I have no reason to think she knows either one of us was not in the house all day. And surely I will have no pleasure in telling anyone what an idiotic, scandalous scrape you almost got yourself into."

Besides, she added to herself, she had no wish to speak about Lord Wolver, as would surely be the case were the events of this afternoon to come under scrutiny.

"Promise me not to do anything like this again," Fenella demanded.

"All right, nothing like this."

As a promise, it lacked substance, but Fenella did not feel she could require more, and the two at last entered the side door of the Manor without undue notice.

To Fenella's surprise, the entire journey to Stockton Priory and back had taken up so little time that no one seemed to know they had been gone.

Even Emma, curiously regarding Charlotte as she hurried up the stairs to her bedchamber, asked no questions of Fenella. The sobs to be heard from behind the locked door of Charlotte's room were proof enough to Emma that Charlotte's elopement had been foiled.

The Fletchers would probably go to London, after all!

10

Not until the day was done, and after being present—although in truth she ate very little—at a dinner *en famille* more tedious than usual, was Fenella allowed to retreat to her bedchamber. She set the lighted candle on a table, latched the door behind her, and stretched her hands out to the welcome warmth from the fire on the hearth. Only then dared she allow herself to consider the day's events, lest in some way her troubled thoughts might appear on her features.

And full of events, the day had been!

Had it not been for Emma, who knows what disastrous news might now be heading toward Chantrey Manor?

Word of the breakdown of the ancient carriage, spilling its occupants along the roadside? Suppose Charlotte had driven away with Dolph Thorne before she got there? There was no doubt that by this hour they would be nearing the Scottish border. It was entirely possible that they would not travel well. The coach did not look sturdy. Surely the years of idleness must have rotted even well-oiled leather, dried the spokes so they did not fit well in the wheels? Fenella would not have trusted her limbs to the hazards of the high road in a vehicle unused since before her own birth!

And if they were forced to spend a night on the road? Charlotte's feverishly romantic state of mind might well have led Dolph to forget Charlotte's station and consider her a prime subject for seduction. And then, were he successful, what would he have done? Left her with the coach and servants and the bill to pay?

Or would the Fletchers have received a message from Scotland, announcing the "anvil nuptials" of as ill-assorted a pair as she could recollect?

Instead, Charlotte had had a supper tray in her room, on the excuse of a severe attack of megrim, and Fenella herself was sinking rapidly into a formidable depression.

She pulled a chair closer to the hearth and sank into it. She let her head fall back till it rested against the high back of the chair. The heat from the fire touched her face in a comforting, gentle caress. Probably she would soon fall asleep, and not a moment too soon, since she realized for the first time how very tired she was.

Too tired, she realized, to marshal her thoughts in good order. Instead, her mind seemed to swing from one remembered scene to another without logical sequence. At length, she let her thoughts drift wherever they would.

Now, thought Fenella, unconsciously, echoing Emma's comment, the family would undoubtedly go to London. She would not necessarily be unemployed, since Sir Eustace wished her to manage the family funds set aside for the visit. Somehow she could not now worry about that.

The face that swam in her mind now was, not Robert's, but that of the arrogant Lord Wolver.

She had not thought to see him again. Nor had she decided how she would feel were he by happenstance to reappear in her life. Now, stunned by his actual appearance, and especially by seeing him under such bizarre circumstances, she did not know how she felt.

He was nothing anymore to her.

Then why was she so depressed?

Sheer shock, of course. Sheer embarrassment at seeing him evolved into an elegant top-of-the-trees sophisticate, while she was a mere governess, well-paid but lowly, scarcely better than a servant. Besides, she did not look at her best. Her bonnet had been awry, her face smudged, and she had scolded Charlotte with more passion than she had ever, as a proper young lady, evinced when Robert held her. She had not thought she had so much of the termagant in her.

She was too tired, too distressed to stir herself to make ready for bed. Instead, she fell asleep in her chair, and

dreamed that Lord Wolver had taken her to London and
thrown her into the lion cage in the Tower.

Had she been able to be present in an invisible state,
Fenella would have enjoyed the discussion at Stockton Priory
after her swift departure.

Lord Wolver had watched her out of sight. Then he turned
to Dolph with a curt nod, and led the way into the house.

Since this was merely a minor manor of his great-uncle's
and thus rarely visited, he had come to stay with his relation
at Stockton Priory only once before, when he was a child.
He had been Robert Thorne then, and he still thought of himself under that name. The title was too recent to sit comfortably on his shoulders.

Now he scarcely noticed the pleasantly spacious rooms,
the scent of beeswax and applewood smoke that spoke of
a well-kept house.

He managed to greet his servants with civility and a smile
which won them completely. "Perhaps you would bring refreshment to us in the . . ." At a loss to know what rooms
there were, he was rescued by the butler.

"There is a good fire in the library, my lord."

"Very well." He glanced at Dolph and added, "I think
tea will be appropriate."

Napier managed not to raise an eyebrow. Tea was not what
he considered a gentleman's drink. But he was relieved, since
young Mr. Thorne had made substantial inroads on the late
earl's cellars in the weeks he had been in residence.

The butler wondered now whether he had done the right
thing in following Mr. Thorne's requests for the good port,
and a bottle of claret every evening with dinner. Mr. Thorne
had told him that the new earl had sent him to take possession
of the house until his cousin had time to make a visit. The
young man's explanation had seemed plausible at the time.

Now, the manner of his lordship toward Mr. Thorne did
not, to the butler's experienced eye, display the confidence
that young Mr. Thorne claimed.

And what Napier was to say when his lordship inspected
the cellars, he did not know!

After tea had been brought to the library, and the door

closed firmly against interruptions, Robert said, "I cannot be sure of the quality of the wine here, so I hesitated to offer any to a man of your experienced palate."

"Our great-uncle's cellars were impeccably laid down, Robert, as you well know! What you mean," said Dolph calmly, "is you fear I'll get drunk. Well, after the turn you served me, I might well do so."

"But not, for the sake of my conscience, on my cellar. How is it that I find you here?"

"Did you not offer me the use of one of your many, many manors? Ah, I see I must have misunderstood you."

"You have been here long, I surmise?"

"Only a month or two," Dolph assured him, without hesitation lopping two months from his stay.

"Long enough, apparently, to insult my neighbors. Certainly your intended bride is gently born. Or did you intend some flummery instead of Gretna?"

Although Robert's voice was pleasant, Dolph was not deceived. He was thankful for a clear conscience, at least on this head. "She's well enough in the pocket," said Dolph. "I could do worse."

Robert raised an eyebrow. "Under the hatches?"

"Of course," said Dolph impatiently. "Why else would I come to this godforsaken country place? Do you know, they tell me they have snow in the winter sufficient to clog the roads for days at a time?"

"At least the Bow Street Runners could not get through to you. What mischief have you got yourself into?"

Dolph turned sullen. "None of your business."

"I shall hope it is not," said Robert pleasantly, "for I have no intention of coming to your rescue again."

"I should think," said Dolph nastily, "that the great earl would care about his reputation."

Robert smiled. "Had Gervase survived the war long enough to inherit, you could be right. But this great earl feels his reputation cannot be badly damaged by a cousin whose qualities are well-known and deplored by those who matter."

Dolph considered his situation. The only source of money possible to him was this cousin who stood before him at this moment, calmly drinking his tea and smiling.

This cousin was too straitlaced for Dolph's taste, and it was perfectly possible that Robert would ride directly to Chantrey Manor and put a spoke in his wheel. Such a turn of events would not suit Dolph in the least.

Therefore it was imperative for Dolph to extricate himself from whatever blame there was in this afternoon's aborted elopement.

"The fair damsel in question," he began with a sardonic air, "seemed to think I was her only hope. Her mother wants to take them all to London, to get Charlotte a husband."

"Charlotte being the naive young lady? Or the chaperon?" Fenella had altered so much that Robert wondered wildly whether she had changed her name.

"Charlotte Fletcher, her name is. And there was no question of a chaperon. Good God, Robert, do you think any duenna would accompany an eloping pair to Scotland? No, the other female is a nosy governess, name of Standish," he finished waspishly.

"You should be thankful you were prevented," said Robert dryly. "Continue."

After a moment Dolph went on. "Charlotte, I fear, clings to me."

"And you say she is an heiress?"

"A substantial one, my sources inform me."

"Well, Dolph, I shall see that this ploy is not successful. After all, the girl seems to be underage. You may see the inside of the Old Bailey yet, for debt or for seduction. The girl's family will not accept you, you know."

"Ah," said Dolph in triumph, "but an unlucky marriage is better than a blasted reputation. Which would be the case, were her grandfather ill-advised enough to refuse me the fortune. And of course the girl."

Robert gazed thoughtfully at him. "I believe you would try that. But if you take my advice—and believe me, if you wish for my favor, you will—you will forget young Miss Charlotte. Out of sight, you know, is out of mind."

"Out of sight?"

Robert seemed surprised at the question. "You are leaving in the morning."

Seeing his hopes fading, Dolph said, "If it hadn't been

for that nosy female, you would have been too late. We should have been gone.''

"Then we must be grateful to Miss Standish.''

"This time, perhaps. But I should urge you not to give surety that the wedding will be forestalled forever by that interfering ape leader!''

The frown on his cousin's face told Dolph he had gone too far this time. He turned the subject quickly. "Don't you have an engagement at your mother's?''

"She is expecting me,'' said Robert, welcoming the diversion. He did not wish to discuss Miss Standish with his cousin. Long accustomed by nature and by his military responsibilities to keep his own counsel, he had not confided in anyone, not even his mother, about his courtship with Fenella Standish.

The conversation fell into less-stressful lines, and at length Robert was left alone to think about the day's events. He was due at Lady Margaret Thorne's country home, only two counties away, for what was announced to him as a quiet family fortnight. However, Robert was willing to place a substantial wager that his mother had a matrimonial prospect lined up for him.

Lady Margaret, excessively fond of her only son, perceived him to be unduly melancholy ever since his return three years before from the war, or at least when he had returned from London that year. Now that he had, against all probability, succeeded to the title, it was more than ever desirable, even imperative, that he marry. Lady Margaret believed it her duty to further this ambition of hers. The past six months, since he inherited, had been a constant procession of marriageable females paraded before him for his scrutiny.

It did no good to chide his mother. Lady Margaret knew what was best for her son, as well as for anyone else who fell beneath her interested gaze.

However, no matter how powerful his mother's claims on him might be, he could not leave Stockton Priory until he had seen Fenella. He had been so astounded at the actual appearance of the lady, who had never entirely left his thoughts, that his wits had gone a-woolgathering.

He did not intend to lose her again.

11

It was a measure of Robert's inexperience with lesser orders that he expected simply to walk into the foyer of Chantrey Manor and ask for one who, while well-paid and highly respected, was nonetheless a mere employee. A visit from Lord Wolver demanded reception by the lady of the house herself.

Before Robert opened his mouth, the butler spoke, much pleased to see a gentleman of such quality, dressed in tasteful country attire, entering the house. "I shall inquire if Mrs. Fletcher is at home." Knowing full well who the visitor must be, he added, "What name shall I say?"

"Wolver," said Robert.

Sophy rose in some confusion when he was announced. The family was gathered in a spacious salon that could, if desired, hold forty persons without crowding. Robert had the impression of wading through surf, so long did it take him to move the length of the room with the gaze of four fascinated females fixed unwaveringly upon him.

When he reached them, and had made his bow over Sophy's hand and been invited to sit, he realized that only three females seemed fascinated by him. The fourth, Fenella, was engrossed in an elaborate and demanding task of sorting out embroidery silks, and did not look at him.

Sophy performed the introductions. "My elder daughter, Charlotte . . . my younger daughter, Emma," she pointed out.

Charlotte was gazing at him with terror in her prominent

brown eyes. He read her thoughts easily. His bland expression as he bowed to acknowledge the introduction gave no hint that he had ever seen her before, and went far to establishing his credit with her.

"And this is Miss Standish," said Sophy without further explanation.

A flicker of amusement passed over Fenella's face. She wondered whether Lord Wolver recognized the alteration in Sophy's voice as she mentioned the governess. However, civility demanded a response from her, and she managed it somehow.

Her thoughts were churning, however. Why was he here? Had he come to expose Charlotte's foiled elopement? And, judging from his attitude at Stockton Priory the previous day, he was not in the least averse to blaming Fenella for the whole coil!

She looked ahead to see herself blamed unjustly for Charlotte's foolishness, her own credit destroyed, and she herself turned off without a reference to trudge the road to the village to take the stage to Nottingham . . . or somewhere. Perhaps they would allow the groom to transport her and her trunk and her recovered bandbox at least as far as the coaching inn!

She returned from these gloomy fantasies to find that Sophy was addressing her in her social voice, much altered from her usual manner.

"Pray inform Sir Eustace that Lord Wolver has called, and ask him to descend."

Robert watched the governess gather her work together and depart, leaving him to the mercies of this impossibly arch Mrs. Fletcher.

He did not afterward remember the tenor of the conversation that followed, save that it was excessively civil and therefore more than ordinarily trivial. His thoughts rambled without any connection to what he was saying.

How did it happen that the very fashionable lady he knew had come to be a governess in this remote and rural area of England? He had been well aware that she was without money, but he had supposed she had relations with whom she could find a home. Besides, she had so thoroughly indicated that she wished *nothing* from him that he could not pursue her.

His reflections were interrupted by the entrance of Sir Eustace, and he rose to greet his host. He saw a man of medium height but more than medium girth, with the sun-burned face of a countryman and a bluff manner to match.

Behind him, unobtrusively, Fenella returned, but sat closer to the door than before, and took out her handwork again.

After a few words of greeting, Sir Eustace said, "I'm mighty pleased to see you, Wolver. I had in mind to mention to you that young relation of yours."

Robert maintained a calm expression, although his spirits sank. Sir Eustace was about to take him to task, and rightly, for Dolph's part in the intended seduction, or marriage, of Sir Eustace's granddaughter. He had no defense, save that of ignorance of the scheme, and he suspected that might not serve him well.

And, he wondered, had Fenella thrown all the blame on Wolver himself, to save her own credit with the Fletchers?

But Sir Eustace was not speaking about his delinquent granddaughter. "Wondered why you sent that fribble down to take over the Priory."

Sophy expostulated, "Sir Eustace!"

"Know he's related to you," he continued, ignoring her. "Wouldn't bring up the matter at all otherwise. Getting him out of the way, eh? Wouldn't blame you."

The tone of Sir Eustace's comment was surprisingly without animosity. Indeed, now that Robert considered it, his welcome had been warm, as he might have expected, knowing that the warmth was for the Earl of Wolver and not for the man Robert Thorne. However, he had expected at least a word on the subject of Dolph's sins and Charlotte's waywardness.

Instead, it was as though the elopement, its planning and its forestalling, had never happened. The family must therefore be ignorant of the entire episode! Well, he certainly was not the one to enlighten them.

But why had not Fenella informed the girl's mother and grandfather? Judging from his own impression of them, their

reactions might be anticipated, and common sense would not
be a guiding factor.

Dryly Robert answered his neighbor's rude query. "I did
not precisely constrain him to come, you know."

From her corner Fenella picked up the rueful amusement
in his voice. In a way, it was comforting to know she still
understood him and was in sympathy with him. At that
moment he caught her eye, and for the smallest moment some
kind of message passed between them. She looked quickly
away, and he believed he must have been mistaken.

"Knew a feller like him once. Cheated at cards. His eyes
too close together too." Sir Eustace sighed and shook his
head, as though in sorrow over the evils of the world.

Eventually Robert realized that Fenella was beyond his
reach this day. Besides, he had stayed overlong for a courtesy
visit, and had not even the excuse of enjoying himself.

When he rose to take his leave, Sir Eustace and Mrs.
Fletcher both urged him to return soon. An invitation to
dinner was spoken of.

After his punctilious leave-taking, Robert let the reins lie
slack in his hand, allowing his pair to trot unhurriedly toward
the Priory. His servants had been prompt in forwarding the
earl's curricle and cattle for his use during the four days he
had intended to stay at the Priory, after which he would again
set his carriage and horses on the road for his mother's home.

He had much to think about at this moment, however,
without refining too much on the joys awaiting him at Lady
Margaret's house party. There would be an eligible heiress
—did Dolph say Lady Hester? . . . an antidote if there ever
was one—and likely many an excursion and charades, if he
were unlucky.

Those delights were for next week, if he did go to Thorne
Abbey. It had not struck him until yesterday that the
possibility of refusal existed.

He called several times at Chantrey Manor. Fenella did
not appear. He must find another means to reach her, for
he needed talk to her, to assure her that his feelings for her
were not changed, and to learn whether there was a chance

for him. The worst that could happen, he thought, would be to find out that she loathed him.

But first he must find out how to reach her in some way short of storming the upper floors of Chantrey Manor by force.

During the next fortnight, Charlotte remained very close to Chantrey Manor. Whether her altered habits were owing to Dolph's absence from the neighborhood—a result of Lord Wolver's unequivocal orders—or because she feared discovery of her past misbehavior was difficult to know.

Charlotte recognized that she had had a narrow escape, but from what, she was not precisely certain. It had been a foolish plan. To elope with a man who had coaxed one with stolen kisses and sugary words at secret meetings was of all things romantic. However, to face the reality of Grandfather's rage and her mother's disappointment, as pointed out by Fenella, was quite another matter.

It did not help that Dolph was not present to restore her spirits, either.

But Charlotte, while foolish, was not stupid. She had given thought to her future, and many things that Dolph had told her came back to her with a significance she had not seen at first.

She was aware of Lord Wolver's importance in Dolph's scheme of things. He had indicated that his wealthy cousin would provide handsomely for him. And of course, Dolph was next in line for the title. Were something to happen to the earl, then Dolph would succeed and she would be Countess of Wolver.

Fenella had told her more than once that social intercourse in London was conducted in line with different rules than prevailed in the more rural areas of England. Considering the shining though vague future that could be hers, she was determined not to shame Dolph.

To Fenella's surprise, Charlotte began to speak of the London trip with some enthusiasm. Any time remaining from

Emma's studies was commandeered by Charlotte, so that
Fenella's days were spent upstairs.

She was not, therefore, aware that Lord Wolver had called
at Chantrey Manor several times in the last fortnight. At none
of his visits had he asked for Fenella, not wishing to make
a point of his interest.

At odd moments, however, when she was sequestered for
the evening in her own room, or even in the small hours of
the night when sleep evaded her, she found herself thinking
of him. She had done well to refuse him, and it was merely
bad luck that he had reappeared in her life.

However, she was not as content with her position here
as once she had been.

Lord Wolver would of course go to London for the Season,
for pleasure and for looking out for a wife.

The Fletchers would accept Lady Crewe's invitation, and
travel to the spacious house on Grosvenor Square, for
pleasure and for looking out for a good match.

And Fenella would sit like a crone in the inglenook,
holding the money! At least, in the chimney corner she would
not have to face her former London acquaintances, except
by chance.

At the end of that fortnight, Fenella made a decision. She
would resign, and go right away from Robert, away from
London. She dared not wait to find a convenient time to
inform Sir Eustace, for she could almost feel her resolve
seeping out through the soles of her slippers.

Upon being bidden to enter the study, she slipped through
the door and approached the big desk behind which Sir
Eustace sat leaning back in his big chair. To her surprise,
his usual frown was replaced at the moment by a broad grin,
and she detected a kind of sly triumph in his little eyes.
"There you are!" he said heartily. "I was about to send for
you."

"Indeed, sir?"

"You'll have to know sooner or later," he told her,
rubbing his hands together.

If he were going to dismiss her, he could find cause only
in the elopement. But who could have informed him?

However, his congenial attitude did not seem compatible with letting a servant go.

"Shall you let me know sooner, then?" Her voice was commendably steady, but her hands moved of themselves in her lap.

"They've decided not to go to London after all!"

She was puzzled. The relations among members of this household had been merely civilized. Warmth and affection were not terms that occurred to her in this regard. The notion that Sir Eustace would not be deprived of the comfort of his daughter-in-law and her children would never in Fenella's opinion lead to such apparent gratification as he now displayed.

"The marriage banns are not far off!" he said.

"Marriage?" she echoed. Charlotte had been silent on the subject. Indeed she had been in the sulks because Dolph was away. And yet, who else? Perhaps Dolph had returned and confessed his part in the elopement, and Sir Eustace considered the marriage an advantage.

Inevitably her thoughts flew to the man not far at any time from her thoughts. Would Lord Wolver give his permission?

"It won't be necessary to take them all to London!"

"Not yours, sir?" Inanely she could not refrain from echoing her employer's words. If not Sir Eustace's duty, then whose? Lady Crewe's?

"Never thought she'd marry again! Not that she wouldn't jump at the notion of getting away from here. Never had a chance, though!"

"I collect you mean Charlotte?"

"Not so. Sophy! Never would have credited it, but there's no mistaking the signs."

Bewildered, Fenella could only shake her head and wait for further enlightenment. She had not long to wait.

"To think that milk-and-water creature could snare the likes of Lord Wolver!"

"Who?"

"Lord Wolver, I tell you. Hasn't spoken to me yet, but Sophy's a widow. Doesn't need my permission, not that I wouldn't give it gladly."

Lord Wolver? *Robert?*

"He's here all the time. Why else would he keep coming?"

"I . . . I had not realized he had been . . . paying his addresses to Mrs. Fletcher."

"Here every couple of days. He can take on paying for all the female fripperies and the trip to London. Matters not a whit to him, you know. Wealthy as a nabob!"

Fenella did not know how she took leave of Sir Eustace.

Whatever she had expected when he summoned her, the news that Lord Wolver had fastened upon Sophy Fletcher was a total surprise.

Nor had she expected that such news would turn her thoughts *bouleversé,* a word she had only an hour before explained to Emma as signifying wrecked, overthrown, convulsed. All of these applied.

She walked without direction. Her feet took her eventually to the rose arbor, and she sat on the wooden seat, surrounded by the dead trunks of the vines that, in another season, would provide a riot of blooms. Now it was still cold and she felt as frozen as though she were a snow maiden.

I must waste no time in resigning, she told herself, get away from here at once.

Robert and Sophy together? She could not endure the thought!

She lost all track of time. The early-spring wind rose and she shivered inside her light wrap. If she took cold, no one would care, but she would not be fortunate enough to take a mortal illness.

The sky was leaden enough to match her mood. Eventually she began to think more clearly, and it occurred to her that if it were true that Lord Wolver found Sophy Fletcher attractive, then she had been grossly mistaken in him. That conclusion went a short way toward restoring her spirits.

She was oblivious of her surroundings. She did not at first hear footsteps approaching along the forest road, opening onto the lawn just beyond the rose arbor.

Only when they stopped a few feet away from her did she notice them. She looked up, startled—into the face of Lord Wolver.

It was too late to flee.

12

Earlier that afternoon, at about the same moment that Fenella had decided to resign her position, Robert stood at the window of the Crimson Salon at Stockton Priory.

The room, furnished as it was in crimson velvet and a great amount of gilt, was not conducive to quiet thought. His memories of Stockton Priory had not included this salon, confined as he had been to juvenile quarters, but he was sure his great-aunt had considered the heavy furnishings as the latest crack.

However, the interior amenities of this house were not the subject of his thoughts this day. He had been in residence here for a fortnight. The estate, while fairly large, was merely one of the secondary estates of which he was now possessed, and other of his lands required his attention. He could have conferred at length with his farm manager, outlined the alternatives he wished made, and left the manager in charge. But he had not done so.

He was in residence alone, save for a number of servants, some of whom he had not even seen.

Robert was overdue at his mother's, and daily expected a messenger carrying a severely scolding message. Who needed a London Season to find a wife when Lady Margaret Thorne conducted her own Marriage Mart?

Why, then, was he still lingering? He suspected he had never fallen out of love with Fenella. He was more deeply in love than he could ever recover from. But there was still mystery here in Fenella Standish. She was undervalued, and

he must know why. He took hope in what he thought were
signs that she was not totally indifferent to him, but he was
not a vain man, and he could not be sure of her feelings.
If he could only talk to her!

He had not had any success in the *tête-à-tête* he longed
for. When he had driven to Chantrey Manor, only Mrs.
Fletcher had been receiving. Sometimes Sir Eustace—that
bombastic idiot—had joined her, and Robert's patience had
often been sorely tried. If he suffered under the tedium that
reigned at the Fletcher household, how much worse must
it be for Fenella? He had already seen that she was not a
downtrodden governess whose spirit had been broken!

Short of storming the castle, so to speak, he did not quite
see his way clear. He could not send her a note, nor could
he without compromising her reputation ask for her. She had
pretended not to know him. Perhaps he had stumbled on the
right key to retrieve his credit? He would start anew with
her, and perhaps their unhappy ending could be erased!

Impatient for action, he left the Priory. This time he
decided to take the forest lane, a shortcut that he believed
would bring him to the buildings at the rear of the manor.

When he emerged from the forest, he realized that at last
his hand was in. The object of his interest was huddled in
the rose arbor, making a figure no larger than a child's. He
stopped a few feet away from her.

She looked up then. At sight of him a faint pink spread
upward from her collar, and she started to her feet.

"Please don't go," he said at once. "I should like to talk
to you."

She sank back on the seat. "Very well, my lord."

After a moment he said, "I had hoped to see you before
this. My behavior some days ago, on the occasion you well
recall, was inexcusable."

On the strength of his unexpected apology, she could be
generous. "There is no need to apologize, Lord Wolver. I
suspect that my own words sounded much like scolding."

"I do not recall them," he said mendaciously. "I suspect
that your charge has since given you no trouble?"

"Charlotte has become quite biddable."

They were silent for a moment. She stirred, and Robert, wishing to detain her, said quickly, "I collect you have not informed the family? When I visited the next day, I quite expected to be called out on behalf of young Dolph!"

How pleasant he was! He seemed to bear her no grudge for her refusal of him. She was becoming quite comfortable with him. She knew she was unbending more with him than her position justified, but she could not help it. Besides, she became aware of a longing to explain to him just how it had come about that she was embroiled in a situation that did none of them any credit.

"She seemed quite overset. I saw no need to bring more punishment down upon her head. Especially"—she smiled suddenly—"since I understand the young man is no longer at Stockton Priory."

"He departed the next day."

"Then I suppose there will be no further danger from that quarter. All that is left me is to deal with Charlotte's willfulness."

"Willfulness!" he exploded. "I should call the young lady perverse, obstinate, unreasonable!"

Fenella laughed. "You may be right."

Encouraged by her laugh, by her obvious easiness in his company, Robert ventured, "How do you fare as governess? You are not what I would expect as a governess. I should think that such a position would be particularly galling to you."

He was much too perceptive. "Galling" was the precise word. But she had counseled herself to endure, to accustom herself to what could not be changed. But only now had anyone recognized the cost she was paying.

"The Fletchers have been very kind to me," she said loyally. "I am comfortable, and little Emma has a sweet disposition, even though she is not inclined to the scholastic life."

Intending only to convey an interest in Fenella's affairs, Robert made a mistake. "I should like to hear what subjects she is learning."

She stiffened. Of course he should like to hear about

Emma's studies! How foolish she had been! Sir Eustace had informed her that the marriage banns would soon be up. Everything Robert—Lord Wolver—had said, all the questions he had asked her, all were part and parcel of his intention to acquire Sophy Fletcher and her daughters as soon as may be.

"I think you must inquire of . . . of Mrs. Fletcher, my lord."

This time she rose abruptly. The hurt in his eyes at her rebuff was clear, but she steeled herself. But she must not give him cause to think her uncivil.

"Perhaps you should go on up to the house," she suggested.

"House? Why?" he demanded, more harshly than he intended.

He looked searchingly at her for a long moment, and then turned away. He took a few steps toward the opening of the forest lane, and then turned back to her.

"You will take a cold if you linger here," he said with such concern that her eyes stung with tears. With an attempt at lightness, he added, "I am sure Mrs. Fletcher will not be willing to take charge of a sickroom!"

Such concern for Sophy was the last straw for Fenella. "Oh, no!" she exploded, seeing him indistinctly through swimming eyes. "She will be much too busy!"

She turned and stumbled toward the house. He watched her out of sight. Then, remembering that he stood in open view of the windows on this side of the house, he hastened for the shelter of the trees.

He should, of course, pay his respects at the house. If anyone saw him at the edge of the lawn, he would be hard pressed to explain why he had come so far and no farther.

At the moment, civility be hanged!

As Robert strode through the Fletcher woodland toward his own boundary, his conversation with Fenella was alive in his mind.

At first she was reserved, aloof, even hostile. He could

not fault her for that, since she had found him not suitable for marriage.

Then, to his gratification, she seemed to consider him harmless. But even as he believed her to be easier with him, she dropped a curtain between them. Suddenly they were strangers. He could not recall precisely what he had said that turned her against him.

At length he reached the tumbling brook that, on its way to the sea, formed the boundary between Fletcher and Wolver. He paused to look out across the valley. From here he could see broad and prosperous fields, tiny houses with smoke curling up into the quiet sky. It was good country, providing a living for those who worked hard, but perhaps a trifle austere.

The lane he was following must have been the way that Dolph and the girl had managed to carry on their secret meetings, hidden from the Fletcher household.

He was not sure whether Dolph's intentions had been honorable—that is, if honorable included marrying a child for her money—or whether he would have seduced her under promise of marriage and then found urgent business elsewhere.

For a startled moment the parallel between his own situation and that of his cousin was blindingly clear. He certainly had journeyed by a secret woodland path, but Fenella was no heiress whose dowry he needed. Quite the contrary. Now he had thoughts only for the pale and prickly lady he had just left.

Unfinished business lay between them, and he would not leave Stockton Priory until it was finished.

He must write to his mother. She had been expecting him for several days now, and she might be worried by his nonappearance.

A brisk five minutes' walk brought him to the rear evirons of the Priory. He took note of the riotous growth of a hedge planted at least three generations ago, and generally held in check. Another item to go on his growing list of needed repairs, he thought.

As he approached the stable area, he became conscious of an unusual stir in the bricked yard. From his vantage point he was struck by the number of grooms busy around a carriage. Surely there were more men than he employed? And the carriage was not his own.

One of the men detached himself from the others and came to him. Robert recognized with a good deal of surprise his mother's coachman.

"My mother's here?" he asked, not believing the evidence of his eyes.

"Yes, my lord."

"In good health?"

"Oh, yes, my lord."

Batton stood unmoving before him. Clearly there was a message to be conveyed, but Robert was not certain what it was. His mother in a temper at his absence? That would not be surprising, nor, he thought, would Batton consider it proper to comment on Lady Margaret's mood.

Good God! Maybe his mother had brought the redoubtable Lady Hester with her! That was outside of enough. Robert, grim-faced, strode to the house to deal with his interfering mother.

He found her completely at home, sitting cozily before the fire in the room Robert called his library. Her feet were extended toward the blaze, and she held a cup of tea in her hand.

She looked at him, a mixture of pleasure and some suspicion in her face. "Robert!" she exclaimed. "I am so relieved to see that you are not abed with a megrim."

"You know I am never ill," Robert said, pleasantly. "You need not have been concerned."

"You think I may not worry about my only child? I cannot wait until you have a son of your own. Then we shall see whether you grow overanxious over the least sniffle!"

He poured a cup of tea for himself and sat down opposite her. "Since that happy prospect is not in sight," he told her, "we shall not know the result, shall we?"

"You do not seem pleased to see me."

"I shall be more than happy to see you, once I discover whether you have brought Lady Hester with you."

"Lady Hester!"

"My cousin told me you had the lady primed for my visit."

"I hope I know better than to bring Hester here. Not but what you could do worse than offer for her. Excellent family."

"I understand the duke has sold his grays at Tattersall's."

"That doesn't mean he is under the hatches!"

He gave his mother a knowing smile.

"Well," she said, "at least she is a duke's daughter!"

"So are you, dear Mama, but you married where you wished. I have the greatest affections for you, but I do wish you would allow me to choose my own wife."

She bristled. "Certainly I would, but you are unconscionably idle on this matter, and I despair of you."

"I shall marry, when I am ready."

"Pooh! You should have been ready long since!"

Robert set his empty cup down and leaned back in his chair. Regarding his mother with slightly raised eyebrows, he murmured, "Why should you take the trouble to visit me here, I wonder. Surely Thorne Abbey would be a better setting in which to set your snare."

Lady Margaret had the grace to blush. "I do not set traps," she said with immense dignity. "I have only your welfare at heart."

"Strangely, considering all the ladies you have persuaded me to meet under one excuse or another, I do believe you. But, dear Mama, you know I should not be happy with any of your prospects."

"You haven't met Hester."

"Nor shall I, willingly."

Lady Margaret shot a suspicious glance at him. "Does that mean you have already fixed your interest?"

He recalled with a start that although he had been ready to offer for Fenella, indeed *had* offered, he had never, knowing his mother's managing propensities, mentioned her name to Lady Margaret.

"I believe I have," he said.

There was a silence between them. A log burned through and fell with a soft plop into the ashes. Lady Margaret finally said, "You may find yourself promised before you know you have offered. I venture the lady is more than willing."

Very slightly, Robert stiffened in his chair. With sudden suspicion, he inquired, "Which lady do you mean?"

Lady Margaret, recognizing the signs of rising temper in her son, hastened to soothe him. "I do not wish to interfere—"

"Someone already has," said Robert. "Let me hazard a guess. Dolph, no doubt. He must have run directly to you."

Avoiding a direct answer, she said, "Of course Dolph's character leaves much to be desired, but he does have the family interest at heart."

Grimly Robert disagreed. "He has *Dolph's* interest uppermost. Will you oblige me and tell me exactly what he said to you?"

Thus urged, Lady Margaret was relieved to share the burden that had lain on her mind since Dolph had sought refuge at Thorne Abbey. "Dolph said you had been paying too much attention to . . . to a lady in this vicinity."

"And I suppose he suggested you would not like her."

"Well, something of the sort."

"Precisely, please." His tone of voice was unyielding.

"He did not slander her," she protested, "so there is no need to call him out!" After a moment she continued on an altered note, "You may ask him yourself."

"He came with you?"

She had been laboring under a guilty conscience, both at coming to Stockton Priory without even sending word ahead, and at bringing young Dolph, whom she knew Robert detested. Striving to justify herself, she said, "What could I do? The boy has no place to go."

"I could wish you had not brought him, especially since I specifically forbade him to return!"

Lady Margaret was shocked. "He did not tell me that!"

"However, all may not be lost. Let him stay. I may find

him useful. However, I trust my presence will serve as a damper on some of his worst inclinations.''

After a moment Lady Margaret said softly, ''Robert, I truly do not mean to be a nuisance . . .''

''You could never be a nuisance, ma'am.''

''But I do hope you will not wed to disoblige me. I should take it hard were my daughter-in-law to be someone I could not like.''

Robert fell silent. In his mind, as clearly as though Fenella were standing before him, he could see her level gaze, her clear gray eyes looking through him, that quality of . . . What? He could not be sure, but it seemed to him very much like vulnerability.

''I believe you may like her,'' he said slowly.

''Then you *have* offered!''

''I think, ma'am, we should probably defer any further discussion of my matrimonial intentions until another day. I suspect I shall someday unburden myself to you in the most juvenile fashion!'' Ruefully he added, ''But . . . not yet.''

''Well, I must be satisfied with that hope, my dear. And truly I am much relieved. I must dress for dinner,'' she said, rising. ''I suspect you keep country hours.'' Upon his nod, she approved. ''Very wise. Much better not to distress the servants unduly by changing their routines.''

She reached the door before he spoke. ''Dear Mama,'' he said softly, ''I'm happy you came.''

Inordinately pleased, she was embarrassed, ''Well, I hope I may be of help to you.''

But you will have an uphill task, she thought, to persuade me to help you win Sophy Fletcher!

13

Lady Margaret was used, from her birth, to having her own way. She had not mellowed in this regard with advancing years. Robert was resigned, therefore, to waiting to be informed by his mother as to what her plans might be.

"I have decided," she told him the next morning, "to stay at Stockton Priory for a month."

"A month?"

"I understand that an old friend of mine is living in this neighborhood, and I shall wish to renew my acquaintance with her. Do you know the Pruitts, Robert?"

"Not at all. I have hardly had the opportunity, since I have been here only a fortnight."

And that fortnight, Lady Margaret thought, was spent in pursuing Sophy Fletcher, from what Dolph said!

"I shall call on Dolly Pruitt this very afternoon, and I shall welcome your company, my dear."

Robert, wary as usual where his mother was concerned, had his excuse ready. "I should like it above all things, but there is a need for me to visit one of the farmers—"

"At the other end of your lands, I suppose," said Lady Margaret, amusement in her eyes. "Very well. I shall take Dolph. He may as well be of some use."

Robert recalled a remark she had spoken only moments before. "A month, you said? Visiting Mrs. Pruitt all the while?"

"Of course not. I shall wish to visit Scarborough, and York Cathedral, and probably Sherwood Forest—"

"All in different directions," murmured her son.

"And perhaps . . . well, all the other sights around. It has been years since I visited here. Your great-uncle preferred other manors to this one." She glanced around her. "Pleasant-enough rooms, I should judge, but I wonder about the winter weather."

"We shall likely never know, ma'am, since I shall take care to avoid the North Country after the first of autumn."

Lady Margaret's visit to her old friend Dolly Pruitt was eminently satisfactory to both ladies. Indeed, Mrs. Pruitt began at once to plan a party to introduce all her neighbors to Lady Margaret.

"Will I have met any of them?" asked Lady Margaret with an air of innocence. "Perhaps in London?"

"I should think not. Most of us here find London so far away as to be no more real than Jerusalem. I have not seen the city since I first came into society." Mrs. Pruitt was silent for a moment, her eyes focused on her own thoughts. "Do you recall that gown I wore—"

"The sea-green satin, of course I do. You never looked more beautiful. Your mother would have been proud."

"I would never give up that memory. But I do enjoy my family, and I should not change it for whatever might have been."

"Tell me the names of your neighbors," urged Lady Margaret, "so that at least I may recognize them when I hear them."

"Well, there's Vicar and Mrs. Roseacre, she was a Temple from Derbyshire, and how she puts up with him, the Lord knows. And there's Sir Walter Clavering—he's the squire . . ."

Mrs. Pruitt continued, but Lady Margaret's interest lapsed after she heard the name she hoped to hear. Sir Eustace Fletcher and his daughter-in-law, Mrs. Fletcher. Lady Margaret believed her maternal instinct could discern precisely her son's interest in a woman she had met once under circumstances she did not recall, had actively disliked, and had no need ever to meet again—until now.

* * *

The invitation to the Pruitts', honoring Lady Margaret, was received at Chantrey Manor with mixed feelings. Sophy was elated.

"What a gala this will be! Mrs. Pruitt knows precisely how matters are arranged," she said to her father-in-law at breakfast. "And to honor Lady Margaret—well, she will outdo herself!"

Sir Eustace took her exclamations with rare good humor. "Stepping up in the world, ain't you?"

"What do you mean, sir?"

"Mother-in-law a duke's daughter!"

"Nothing of the sort!" Sophy protested, but she did not claim ignorance of his meaning. "I am sure her position has nothing to do with me."

"With Wolver practically living on my doorstep? He surely has no eye for Charlotte!" On reflection, he added, "I shouldn't let him have her either. Too old for her. Not for you, on the other hand—"

"Sir Eustace, you are teasing me abominably!"

He was, indeed, and he was enjoying himself. He was more than half-serious, as well, and his boasting to Fenella about Wolver's taking Sophy and the girls off his hands had, in his mind, so much truth in it that he was well on his way to convincing himself that Wolver would soon offer for the woman.

"Mark my words, Sophy, Wolver's brought his mother down to make your acquaintance."

"He has said nothing out of the way to me. He has not even allowed himself the gallantries that I should expect from a London gentleman." Her tone was wistful.

Sir Eustace laughed loudly. "Of course not! You're no giddy schoolroom miss. Besides, you're all too eager. Why should he flirt?"

Sophy was wounded. In a stiff manner she said, "I presume that as usual I must make excuses for you?"

"Certainly not. It would be very uncivil to the duke's daughter not to attend. But I warn you, I'm taking my curricle. I don't want to wait around for all you females when I've had enough."

In due time, the Chantrey Manor party was assembled, the coach and four was brought around to the entrance, and Fenella followed Sophy and the girls into the vehicle.

Fenella did not want to go. She had told Sophy that her own presence at a party where the Misses Fletcher would be under the eye of their mother was not required.

"I wish you to go," Sophy said. "I shall not have time to chaperon them. I shall not wish to be lacking in attention to the guest of honor."

As the carriage rumbled over the roads on the way to the Pruitts', Fenella looked forward to the day with some trepidation. She had not met Lord Wolver—as she insisted on calling him, to maintain her proper distance—in company, save for the first visit he made to Chantrey Manor. She must make sure she did not let her former life overrule the present. She was not meeting Lady Margaret, Lord Wolver, or even Mrs. Pruitt as a social equal.

By the time they had reached the sweep before the Pruitts' entrance, she had decided she had nothing to worry about. Lady Margaret in particular would take no notice of an underling, and surely a cat, Fenella, could look at a king, Lord Wolver, without compromising her situation.

The Fletchers found they were the last comers. Mrs. Pruitt greeted them all kindly, and sent Charlotte and Emma upstairs to join Fanny in the schoolroom. Charlotte went reluctantly, but Mrs. Pruitt insisted, and brought Fenella in to meet the other guests.

Sophy had been presented to Lady Margaret a few moments before Fenella arrived, and already she was in spirited conversation with her. Lady Margaret was enthroned in state at one end of the drawing room, with a smaller chair drawn up at either side, one of which was occupied by a smiling Sophy.

Fenella cast a cautious glance at Lady Margaret, and was relieved to see that she had never met that lady. Fenella was not anxious to meet anyone from the past.

Save of course for Lord Wolver!

But now Fenella did not wish to see him. Yet she realized

that her glance traveled swiftly into all corners of the two rooms, and she knew that she was searching for him.

In the meantime, Lady Margaret was trying to like Sophy Fletcher. It was not easy. The woman prattled on about nonsensical things, and Lady Margaret's mind wandered, as did her gaze. Her attention was arrested when she caught sight of a young woman in the doorway. Somewhere she had seen that woman before, hadn't she?

Whoever she was, she was not the vicar's wife, nor the squire's lady, therefore an unknown. However, the unknown had a certain elegance even in the way she stood, and a sudden doubt rose in Lady Margaret's mind.

Since she had paid no heed to Sophy's conversation, she was scarcely aware that she interrupted her. "Tell me, Mrs. Fletcher, are there others in your household?"

Taken aback, yet insensitive as always, Sophy took the question as a likely inquiry from a prospective mother-in-law. "Well, of course, my lady, there is my elder daughter, Charlotte, who may be coming out in society this year. And a daughter, Emma, who is twelve years old. And of course Emma has a governess."

"Governess?" Good God, thought Lady Margaret, can Robert be toying with a *governess*? At least Sophy was well-bred enough, even though Robert would be bored in a week with her. As Lady Margaret was bored with her now, after only half an hour of her company!

"I thought it best to insist that she come with us today. She will keep an eye on the children. But I confess I do enjoy her company in the evenings when I am alone. She is most amiable and does not object in the least to doing errands or playing piquet to beguile the time."

After, of course, thought Lady Margaret, having spent the entire day teaching.

The afternoon was drawing late. The bountiful dinner had been served and eaten, the little girls had been brought down to make their curtsies, and Sir Eustace, as was expected, had already departed. It would soon be time for them all to leave.

Sophy would not nurse Fenella were she to get a cold! That was all Robert said. And Fenella, like the idiot she was, flung at him some remark full of resentment. And what had Lord Wolver's matrimonial plans to do with her? She had had her chance!

Fenella had been presented sometime that afternoon to Lady Margaret, who had looked directly at her for a long moment and then said a civil word of dismissal. At least she had not seemed to recognize Fenella.

In this conclusion, Fenella was incorrect. After she curtsied and left, murmuring an excuse about seeing to young Emma, Lady Margaret turned thoughtful. She could look kindly now upon Sophy, as she did, realizing that Sophy Fletcher would never be in a position to nettle her. Dolph had been wide of the mark if he thought Robert was hanging out for Mrs. Fletcher. No, Lady Margaret thought, she knew where the truth lay, and at least the girl was a lady.

Fenella had caught Lord Wolver's eye once, as well, but across the width of the room, and there was no opportunity for speech.

Only another hour, she thought, and they would be in the carriage on their way back to Chantrey Manor. She must warn her charges that the time for departure was drawing near. She found Emma and Fanny quietly playing cards upstairs. When she came down again, she realized she had not seen Charlotte for some time.

Her thoughts leapt swiftly to Dolph Thorne. He had kept himself in the background throughout the day, and now he was completely out of sight.

Unobtrusively she drifted through the rooms, looking for either one. At length, near the door to the conservatory, she caught sight of movement. Dolph was leaving the far conservatory door. And Charlotte, unaware of Fenella's presence, slipped through the near door, and bumped into Fenella.

"Oh!" said Charlotte, summoning up a smile. "Were you looking for me? Is it time to leave?"

Fenella studied the girl. "I wonder how you came to disappear from sight, Charlotte?"

"I've done nothing!"

"I shall hope so. I admit I should be less reluctant to believe you had I not seen young Mr. Thorne leaving by the other door."

"We did nothing!"

"Even if you do not know better, Mr. Thorne should not have taken you out of company."

"But we were just in the conservatory, Fenella!"

Fenella looked long at her. "Whether or not, Charlotte, Mr. Thorne committed the least impropriety with you, you cannot believe your absence went unnoticed. I need scarcely remind you that scandal grows as it runs, and you may find that your reputation has gone before you. You really cannot count on my silence on this head any longer."

Charlotte protested. "But we only . . . talked! You wouldn't understand, Fenella. You've never been in love!"

Fenella did not feel she wished to respond to that accusation. In a bracing tone she agreed. "As you have told me more than once. If love turns one giddy as a peahen, then I rejoice that I have not."

The tears brimming in the girl's eyes and her quivering lips told Fenella that she would be fortunate if Charlotte did not give way to hysterics the next moment. She did not need such a scene.

"Very well," she said. "But your behavior is revolting. And I promise you that the next time—mind, Charlotte, the very next time—I shall consider it my duty to speak to your grandfather."

"He'll never let me see Dolph again!"

Fenella could not think that eventuality would be an unrelieved disaster, but wisely she kept silent."

"All right, Charlotte. Go upstairs. Is there a back way through the kitchen? And wash your face. Maybe your mother won't notice you've been crying."

As they had talked, they had moved closer to the conservatory door. Now the heady green scent of moist earth and growing things reached Fenella, and beckoned her. Without thinking, she slipped through the door into the conservatory. She was sure she had not been seen, and she would never be missed by Mrs. Pruitt's guests.

* * *

Surely it would not be wrong to rest for a moment?

The sun through the glass roof drew moisture from the damp earth, so that the air was tropical. She stepped slowly along the brick floor to the midpoint of the conservatory, where she found a pair of chairs drawn close together. She frowned. Charlotte had said nothing happened, but Fenella must be excused for doubting the girl.

Fenella hesitated, then sat in one of the chairs. Her head fitted comfortably against the back of the chair, and she closed her eyes. Why was she so tired? It did not do to pursue that question. Instead she would take five minutes to rest; then she must return to her duties.

She might have drowsed. Certainly she was startled to realize that the fecund smell of wet warm earth had been overlaid by the clean scent of shaving soap. She opened her eyes.

Lord Wolver himself stood only a few steps away. She started to rise.

"Pray stay where you are, Miss Standish. I would not disturb you for the world."

She leaned back and looked up at him.

With some amusement he said, "I should of course start this conversation with a remark about what a fine jungle growth we find ourselves in."

Unsettled by his presence, she did not know how to react.

"R-really, my lord," she said finally, "there is no need for a conversation at all."

"I cannot agree. There is every need. We have many misunderstandings to clear up."

"I do not perceive any. But it would be unbecoming to fence with you, Lord Wolver."

"Unbecoming?"

"Of course, considering the difference in our stations."

"Let us overlook such a paltry objection."

"You may. I cannot." To emphasize her protest, she rose to her feet. "I must go back to Mrs. Fletcher."

He stood unmoving in the aisle. Here in this enclosed space, she realized again how very tall he was, how broad of shoulder . . . She dared not continue in that vein.

"You came in," he pointed out, "for a few moments' respite. Let me stay and fend off intruders."

"I came after Charlotte and . . . that young rake!" She recalled that she was speaking to the rake's near relative. "I beg your pardon."

"Not at all. You speak only the truth."

"How can I prevent them from meeting?"

Thoughtfully he suggested, "Dolph may be agreeable to a separation, if I make it profitable for him."

She understood him. "But why should you put out of pocket? She is foolishly childish, and I cannot for the life of me see her appeal."

"Can't you? Sometimes one's vision is commanded by necessity. Or what one believes to be necessary."

"Oh, yes, I understand that only too well."

A shadow passed over her face, making her seem exceptionally vulnerable, and very fragile. That was a moment of revelation for him. As though illuminated by a great light, in an instant he understood his restlessness, his boredom with the rounds of society in London, his resistance to all his mother's exhibits. He regretted that he had not stormed Oakhurst and carried her off, willy-nilly!

He was shaken by strong emotion as though by an earthquake. How could he have thought he was beyond the reach of passion?

But could she still care for him?

At this moment he was sorely tempted to hazard his future and offer marriage to her then and there. But he noticed the weariness around her eyes and knew decidedly the time was not right. At least he could see that she did not return overly soon to her duties.

"May I sit for a moment?" he suggested, touching her arm. More comfortable then, he said, "I have little knowledge of governesses, since I am an only child. But it seems to me that such a post must be scarcely better than that of housekeeper."

She smiled. "Sometimes not even so well-regarded as that."

"I regret . . . all that has happened to you. I thought you

had relations to come to your rescue. Certainly I could not.''

"No. I see that.''

"But I should have inquired, and made sure you were all right.''

"No need to tease yourself, my lord. What's done is done, and you at least have a happy prospect ahead.''

He could not decipher her meaning, but he persisted. "As a rule, what is done may be undone, you know.''

She wished he were not so close to her. She wished he were not paying court to Sophy Fletcher. She wished he would take her in his arms and let her sob the past three years away on his shoulder.

She said, "May I wish you happy?''

He was startled. Did she too regret her refusal? He devoutly hoped that was true. But he dared not put a foot wrong, not this time.

"That depends.''

"Oh, I think you may expect a happy outcome, my lord,'' she said, hoping she did not sound as waspish as she felt.

She made as though to leave, but Lord Wolver held her wrist tightly in his fingers. "When may I see you?'' he demanded.

"Never. Not at all.''

"We have much to talk of.''

She shook her head. "Nothing.''

"I shall wish to gain your approval for certain arrangements I have in mind for my young cousin Dolph.''

He had not released her wrist, and she suspected he did not intend to let her go until he was satisfied with her answer.

In a very low voice she said, "There is a walk beyond the orchard at Chantrey. It is lovely in late afternoon.''

He lifted her hand to his lips and kissed her fingers. He smiled at her as he released her, and watched after her as she hurried out of the conservatory.

He realized, three years too late, that he did not understand women. He suspected he and Fenella had been speaking at cross-purposes, but how could he get the matter straightened out?

He had told his mother he would confide in her one day. Now it was time.

14

Lady Margaret Thorne, even though she was left a widow when her only son was still at Eton, had most commendably refrained from giving way to Robert's every whim. Nor had she urged him, at least immoderately, in the ways she wished him to go.

On the other hand, she held an extreme devotion to him, and knew well his vagaries of mood. She had read him aright when she first arrived at Stockton Priory a few days ago. There was something—or someone—here who had kept him from his pledge to join her house party. Fortunately, or so she thought at the time, Robert's cousin Rudolph had come straightaway to her to explain her son's absence.

"No marriageable female in sight there," Dolph had told her. "A gaggle of schoolroom misses for the most part." He conveniently overlooked Charlotte, for his own activities in that sphere could be condemned by the more straitlaced of his relations. However, his ambition was to return to Stockton Priory and pursue the heiress, in traditional fashion if it must be, and he believed he knew how Robert's prohibition might be evaded.

"I can't think," said Lady Margaret, "that Robert would have the least interest in schoolgirls. His complaint of all the young ladies I have introduced is that they are empty-headed ninnyhammers. No, there is nothing in that line that keeps him away."

Dolph appeared to be lost in thought. Finally he said, with design and untruth, "There is the widow, of course. Perhaps my cousin . . . Oh, no, that can't be true."

Lady Margaret was at once alert. "Widow? I know of no widow living in that area. The daughter of my old friend lives near Stockton Priory—perhaps you know her? Dolly Pruitt?"

Dolph remembered her well, since he had spent a good deal of time avoiding her.

"Surely Mr. Pruitt has not died? I should have heard if that were so," said Lady Margaret.

"Not Mrs. Pruitt. I daresay you would not know the lady I speak of, Mrs. Fletcher."

"Not Sir Eustace Fletcher's daughter-in-law? Is she widowed?"

"Some years since, I gather. Do you know the lady?" Dolph hung on her answer. He believed that Charlotte's mother was rather more vulgar than Lady Margaret would like, and the surest way for him to return to Stockton Priory would be in Lady Margaret's train as she visited her son.

Lady Margaret's features had lost their pleasant aspect. "I know the lady," she said in a tone that bordered on sternness. After a moment she said, "I think it is time I visited my son. I shall welcome your escort, Dolph."

If Dolph were inwardly rejoicing at the success of his scheme, he did not reveal it. He said only, "As you wish, Aunt."

As Dolph, returning to the place where his fortune lay, was satisfied, so, after the party at the Pruitts', was Lady Margaret herself content. She knew, within moments after all the guests had been introduced to her, which lady had captured Robert's interest, at least for the moment. It was not that foolish woman Sophy Fletcher. Dolph had been wide of the mark there.

But a governess?

Lady Margaret's memory teased her. The governess had been introduced to her by Mrs. Fletcher—who had stuck to her like a plaster!—but although Lady Margaret would never admit it, her hearing was less acute than in her earlier years, and she did not hear the name clearly.

Yet there was something about the face that struck a chord

of memory. How unfair that memory did not also provide her with the name that applied!

After breakfast on the morning after the Pruitts' party, Robert invited his mother into the library and closed the door. Leading her to a chair next to the fireplace, he sat down opposite.

"Robert, such precautions! Are you about to reveal another Guy Fawkes plot?"

"Nothing so exciting, I confess. But I do not wish Dolph to overhear, for he takes too much upon himself as it is. Even he would not stoop to listen in the hallway, where the servants might come upon him."

For once she waited for him to open the subject that obviously weighed heavily on his mind. But when he spoke, she was startled.

"Who *are* the Standishes?"

"*That's* . . ."

He lifted an eyebrow inquiringly. "That's what?"

"That's who she is. Fenella Standish. I should have recognized her."

Exasperated, he said, "Then if you know her, why did you not bring her to those interminable house parties? Instead of Lady Hester, for example."

"Because I was not acquainted with her. I meant that her resemblance to her mother is striking, and her mother I knew very well at one time. That Fletcher woman mumbled her name, and I could not quite remember precisely how I knew the young lady."

"Standish," repeated Robert. "How is it that she comes to be a governess to those abominable children?"

"I could not say. But surely you remember the Standishes? Near neighbors to your great-uncle Wolver. But then, by the time we visited there, my friend Althea had died, and the earl's health had begun to fail, so we did not see them."

"When I knew her . . ." He glanced at his mother. Irreverently he thought she looked curious as a terrier at a badger hole. Firmly he suppressed the notion. But he knew she would not be satisfied until she had heard the whole.

He told her.

Lady Margaret leaned back in her chair. Gratified that her son trusted her in this matter of his heart, and totally allied with him in his desire to marry the daughter of her old friend, she sighed happily. She said, "She has such a look of her mother. I vow I like her much better than your Sophy Fletcher!"

He was startled. "Fletcher! Ma'am pray have a little respect for my intelligence!"

"I am much relieved."

He eyed her suspiciously. "There is no need to involve yourself, you know. Simply advise me how to go on."

Meekly she said, "You remember I promised not to interfere."

He rose and held out his hand to help her from her chair. "Somehow I wonder whether you would have kept that promise had it been a question of Mrs. Fletcher?"

She spoke with immense dignity. "I have more respect for your intelligence!"

He laughed, and left the library.

Late in the afternoon, Robert was pacing the walkway beyond the Chantrey orchard. The grass was scythed, but not close-cut, and not many ladies would find it an attractive walk. Further, it was out of sight of the great house. The measure, he decided, of the isolation of this favorite haunt of Fenella's was the measure of her unhappiness in her situation.

He had walked for the better part of half an hour, back and forth, casting anxious glances toward the path by which she must come, before her neat figure appeared, hastening in his direction.

He went to meet her, hands outstretched. As she approached him, she bent and set down the dog she was carrying. She gave Robert both hands, and he lifted one after the other to his lips.

"I feared you were not coming," he told her.

A frown appeared briefly on her forehead. "Did you? I nearly didn't. We really have nothing to discuss."

"As I told you, we have much to talk of. Three years to catch up on."

"Three years. But truly you are mistaken. We are no longer . . ." Her voice trailed away.

"Betrothed. I am acutely aware of that. But that is no reason for us to rip up at each other." He waited, but she would not meet his eyes. "Come, Fenella. Can we not start anew? I seem to recall you were to teach me to overcome my rough Portuguese ways."

She managed a small smile. "I suspect you have learned much in these three years!"

"I have indeed," he said with such warm intimacy that she turned away lest her expression betray her.

"But you have nothing to fear," he added in mock solemnity. "I shall now behave with the utmost propriety."

She looked away. Muggins had discovered an interesting small creature scurrying to shelter in the tall hedge that screened the fields beyond and ended at the beginning of the home woods. He was burrowing fiercely, uttering small threatening yelps.

She was prevented from scolding him by the gentleman who was offering her his arm. "I think we must walk, else you become chilled."

She must forestall any further expression of interest on his part. While she felt herself still a proud Standish, as wellborn as any earl, she was acutely conscious of her present condition. While she might remember with some pleasure his remark the night of the storm—"I shan't seduce you here on the doorstep of Almack's . . . Perhaps another time"— and certain other incidents during their brief time together, she dared not give way to what Mrs. Fletcher, or even dear Miss Waite, would call loose behavior.

If she had learned one thing in her life, it was that earls did not stoop to governesses. And employers were usually excessively straitlaced.

But just the same, it was pleasant to feel again the hard

muscles of his arm against her, and to look up into his smiling face—and it was at that moment that she recalled that Sir Eustace had told her that the Earl of Wolver was probably going to offer for Sophy!

She tried to pull away, but he prevented her. She was sadly lacking in willpower, she thought, but she had met him here, and certainly civility demanded that she remain, at least for a few moments. The fact that her wishes coincided with the proper thing to do was mere happenstance!

"I should tell you at once that my mother was delighted to meet you yesterday."

"I thought she knew me. But I cannot recall where we met."

"She tells me she recognized your mother in you. She was very fond of your mother."

"So was I," said Fenella quietly. "But I don't remember her very well. She died when I was quite young."

"I would be interested to hear what has happened to you since . . . since we parted."

"Very little to tell," she said with finality. She dreaded to appear self-pitying, and fortunately he did not press her.

They walked in silence for a few moments. The day was turning toward evening, and the sun had already set, sending streamers of crimson and green toward the zenith. They could have been alone in the world.

Somewhere not far off a stick snapped. She was startled, but Robert patted her arm reassuringly. "That foolish dog of yours, doubtless."

He whistled up Muggins for her, and she picked the dog up and tucked him into the crook of her left arm.

"Shall I see you here tomorrow?" he asked.

"I cannot tell. Often I am prevented."

"Then I shall live in hopes. I shall be here."

She smiled, and turned to hurry toward the house.

He watched her out of sight—on her way to safety. He knew that stick had not been snapped by the weight of a dog the size of Muggins!

Fenella reached her room without encountering any of the

family. She had insisted from the beginning on her daily need for proper exercise, so at the end of the day she was for the most part free to follow her own pursuits.

She drew near to the fire—thank goodness Sir Eustace was generous with firewood—and stretched her hands out to the heat. She had indeed become chilled, as Lord Wolver had predicted, but she had not noticed the cold while in his company.

There was, of course, the question of Sophy Fletcher to be considered. Sir Eustace considered Lord Wolver very near offering for her. "Must be," Sir Eustace had crowed. "Why else would he come calling nearly every day?"

Fenella was prepared to hear the news any moment, difficult as it was to understand. This afternoon Lord Wolver had given no sign of being attached to anyone. Indeed, he had spoken as though he had more than a passing interest in renewing his attachment to her.

If it happened that he married Sophy and they left Chantrey Manor for other parts, she would be resigned. But she would have a pleasant interlude to remember. She was, she realized ruefully, not resigned to thinking like a governess. She had been a Standish too long.

She had once lived in the future, so to speak. A happy future had lain ahead of her—marriage, children, the kind of life that any young lady of fortune and family might expect. And that future had vanished overnight.

Now she was determined to live in the present, to enjoy what small pleasures came her way now, since the future could easily hold even more unhappiness than so far had come her way.

She would make her way as often as she could to the walkway beyond the orchard. She hoped devoutly that Robert would be waiting for her there.

Sophy Fletcher, no longer ago than a fortnight, had been determined to take her daughters to London. She had braved the anger of her father-in-law, written to Lady Crewe, and persisted in her arguments until Sir Eustace's resistance was fading.

That evening, at supper served *en famille,* Sophy informed her family that she had changed her mind.

"Not going to London?" roared Sir Eustace. "Good God, I can't fathom you women. First you make my life miserable whining to go, and now the trip is off. What do you mean by this?"

Fenella would have shrunk from listening to family discord of this magnitude, had it not been that Sir Eustace favored her with a wink that Sophy did not see.

"I wonder at you, Sir Eustace," said his daughter-in-law, "for I should think you would recognize that it would be the height of incivility to leave the neighborhood while Lady Margaret is still here."

Sophy glanced at Sir Eustace to see what effect her words had on him. None at all, Fenella judged.

"It's not Lady Margaret," he said. "It's Wolver himself. I have eyes in my head." Perversely bent on teasing her, he added, "I suppose you think he's calling on you when he haunts my drawing room here. Did you think he might be after Charlotte?"

Sophy blushed. "I should not let him marry her."

"Oho! I should think the proper way to protest," said Sir Eustace, enjoying himself hugely, "would be to say you would not allow *her* to marry *him.* But I suppose you have more influence with Lord Wolver than you have with your own daughter." Turning to Fenella, he continued, "I thought you were going to teach the girl how to go on in society, Miss Standish?"

Fenella was prevented from answering. Charlotte burst out, "I don't need to know any more! Mama, why aren't we going to London?"

Sophy, beleaguered, flushed. Fenella's spirits dropped. Was the announcement of Sophy's betrothal to Lord Wolver coming so soon?

"I have told you, Charlotte. It would be most uncivil of me to leave while Lady Margaret is still in residence at Stockton Priory."

"And while Wolver has not come up to the mark," Sir Eustace pointed out crudely.

"I want to go to London!" Charlotte burst out. She shoved her chair back and left the room abruptly. Those left at the table could hear her sobs as she fled upstairs.

At last Sir Eustace said sourly, "Miss Standish, my apologies. I hoped you would instill at least the rudiments of civilized behavior into my spoiled granddaughter. However, even you cannot work miracles." He left the table. At the door he turned and said to Sophy, "Why I ever let my son marry into your family, I cannot conceive. That chit of a girl is the image of your mother—windy in the head."

After he had gone, Sophy glanced uneasily at Fenella. "Pray do not heed Sir Eustace. He seems ill-natured for the most part, but I do not refine upon it." She rose. "I must go to Charlotte."

Fenella suspected shrewdly that Sophy had heard many worse assessments of her family during the years she had been constrained to live at Chantrey Manor. But she could have burst into song—Lord Wolver had not, according to Sir Eustace, offered for Sophy. And Fenella was free to enjoy his company, merely for the moment's pleasure. For earls did not offer for governesses.

Emma had made the most of the family's turmoil at dinner. The last of her trifle was still in her mouth, but she told Shipley, "I'll have Charlotte's sweet, if you please."

When Shipley had gone, and only Fenella kept Emma company at the table, Fenella's curiosity overcame her. "For weeks now," she said to Emma, "Charlotte has refused even to consider going to London. I do not understand why she has so abruptly changed her mind."

Emma obliged. "Dolph's going to marry her in London. Lord Wolver won't let him offer for her here."

15

Dolph Thorne had led, in his twenty-three years, a somewhat checkered existence. His father, the younger brother of Robert's father, had died early, of causes that, considering his life of dissipation and poverty, could be considered natural.

Dolph had inherited his father's enmity toward the rest of the Thorne family, believing they should have provided funds to replace those his father had squandered. Since the Thorne family stood firm against this concept of their duty, Dolph was forced to live by his wits. It was a measure of the family affection for him that no one inquired as to his welfare.

Dolph's wits had led him into strange byways. He had done things he regretted, and many he did not. The one constant in his mind was that his best hope for the future lay in marrying an heiress, preferably a biddable one who would ask no questions, like Charlotte. His second avenue was to cajole a pension from his wealthy cousin. Neither plan would come to fruition if certain activities in his past were to come to light, and he was determined that no questions be raised nor inquiries set on foot.

He had become skillful in moving silently, in eavesdropping without detection, an art he found useful. He had overheard, for example, the revealing conversation of his cousin and Lady Margaret, when they thought themselves private. So the governess who had played him such an evil trick by forestalling his acquisition of Charlotte's fortune was Miss Standish, from the south of England!

That discovery brought him certain unpleasant memories he had thought buried forever. And they must stay buried forever, come what may.

Nor was his stealthy skill confined to interior eavesdropping. The other day, when he had followed Robert down the forest road, he had stepped unwarily. Fortunately Robert did not appear to have heard the snap of the twig under Dolph's foot, and the latter retreated hastily.

In addition, because of the governess's intervention in his elopement scheme, his cousin, taking her side against his own family, had told him he was no longer welcome at Stockton Priory. It did not suit Dolph's purpose to defy him, at least overtly. Lady Margaret had brought him with her, and he was again in a position to lay siege to his heiress.

But Miss Standish stood directly in his way. And Miss Standish was a mere female, and therefore easily threatened.

A few days after the party at the Pruitts', Lady Margaret was surprised when Napier announced Mrs. Fletcher. Sophy followed on the heels of the butler and tripped across the salon to her hostess.

After a few civil words of greeting, and a request for refreshments to be brought, Lady Margaret gazed at her caller with an inquisitive eye and waited to be informed of the purpose for her visit.

Sophy, intimidated by Lady Margaret's manner, was flustered, but went gamely ahead. "I hope you won't think it dreadful of me to call, but as your nearest neighbor I thought it my duty to see how you go on."

"Truly," said Lady Margaret in the sweet voice that would have sounded alarms in her intimates, "I am not your neighbor at all. That honor belongs to my son."

Sophy wisely did not reply to that statement. "I recall that you spoke the other day at Mrs. Pruitts' of wishing to see some of the sights of the country before returning home. I should like to make up a small party for this purpose. I suppose I know the countryside as well as anyone, for you must know the Fletchers have lived in Chantrey Manor for generations."

Lady Margaret recognized the claim of the Fletchers on her. One did not snub the old county families, no matter how much one disliked the present representative sitting opposite her.

"I should not like to trouble you," she said.

"I should count it a pleasure," Sophy told her. "There are several notable sites which may interest you. I believe you mentioned Scarborough?"

Snatching at straws, Lady Margaret denied any interest in the seashore at this time of the year. "Much too cold," she pointed out. "The North Sea winds are particularly bad for my health. Much too far for a day's outing, too. I do not know what I could have been thinking of."

She underestimated Sophy's powers of invention. At last the date was fixed for three days hence, the destination to be Nottingham, where there stood a famous statue of Robin Hood as well as the castle and a church of some note.

"Robin Hood and Maid Marian were married in that very church," said Sophy. "So romantic, you know!"

Since Lady Margaret doubted that the outlaw ever found time to wed, she was not moved. "Who will make up the party? Mrs. Pruitt, of course, and the vicar and Mrs. Roseacre must not be overlooked . . ."

Since Sophy had intended a very private party, with Lord Wolver and his mother only, she saw with dismay her small party growing apace. But she put a good face on her disappointment, and was able to smile at Lord Wolver when he entered.

"Lady Margaret and I," said Sophy archly, "are planning the most delightful excursion! You must not spend all your time with your manager, you know. I know you will particularly enjoy the day."

"Shall I?" Warily he inquired, "For what day do you plan?"

"Three days hence."

"Too bad! I should enjoy it, I feel certain, save that I shall be unable to accompany you."

He was aware that Lady Margaret was sending him an urgent message, but since the last thing he wanted to do, three days hence or at any time, was spend time with the most empty-headed female it had been his misfortune to meet, he did not meet his mother's eye.

"You cannot? I collect a fixed engagement that cannot be broken. Very well, Lord Wolver, are you free the next day? Or the next? Pray set a date, and I shall arrange accordingly."

Robert was no fool. He recognized that the excursion would take place at his convenience, and there would be no avoiding it without insulting his nearest neighbor. He gave in with good grace. "Perhaps three days hence will be best after all."

And be done with it, he thought.

Sophy was elated. She believed that he had altered his plans so as to join the projected excursion, for no other reason than to be in company with her. Sir Eustace might scoff and tell her she would never bring him up to the mark, but surely Lord Wolver distinguished her by his attention. Sophy did not remember that she had been out of society for so long that she might mistake the merest courtesy for a more intimate interest.

The party was made up before Sophy departed. In addition to Lord Wolver and his mother, Mr. and Mrs. Pruitt would be invited. The vicar and his lady, Sir Walter and Lady Clavering.

"And of course the children," said Lord Wolver, astonishing his mother. "Young Miss Pruitt, and the Fletcher young ladies—I suspect such an excursion would be of great educational value." Lady Margaraet, understanding Robert's ploy, added cordially, "Of course it would. I am sure the governess—what is her name?—would be glad of the opportunity for instruction . . . the actual castle to look at, you know."

Her plans altered, but not canceled, Sophy departed. Robert and his mother exchanged a long look.

"You should have realized from the outset, Robert," said Lady Margaret, "that the woman was determined to snare you for her little trip. I was certain she would sit here mentioning day after day until time for dinner. I was much relieved when you capitulated."

Ruefully he said, "There was nothing else to do. I wish I had understood that you were serious about viewing the sights of the area. I should have found time to escort you."

"Good God, Robert, you cannot think I had anything to do with this? No, Mrs. Fletcher picked up a bit of idle conversation from our day at Dolly Pruitt's party and built herself an entire edifice on it."

"Well, we now have no choice in the matter. But I shall drive my curricle, so as to return home early if I wish."

Lady Margaret smiled slyly. "Do you think the governess will ride with you?"

"You caught that?"

"Indeed I abetted your scheme. You are a devious man, Robert."

"All my scheming, ma'am, I learned from you!"

After some time, Robert exclaimed, "I forgot Dolph! Did you manage to exclude him?"

"No, I did not try. Why should I deny the boy the pleasure of an outing to Robin Hood's old haunts?"

"Is that where we are going? I don't remember being informed as to our destination. But perhaps it is better to make Dolph one of the party."

"I don't understand."

"I did not intend to tell you the scene that met my eyes when I arrived at the Priory. However, it is right that you should know. Great-aunt's traveling chariot stood in the yard, with all the servants milling around, like Gulliver and the Lilliputians."

"Aunt Mathilda's chariot? I thought that fallen to pieces an age ago."

"No, it's been kept in excellent shape, although I should not wish to entrust my bones in it over the road. The leathers must be thirty years old at least. The servants seemed to be in the process of roping ill-assorted luggage to the roof."

"Were they decamping with the furniture?"

"Much worse. Dolph was roaring at them to hurry, and two young ladies seemed to be at odds in the foreground."

"You seem to see it as a scene in a play."

"And so it seemed to me at the start. Rather a set piece,

you know. The Priory in the background, the forest behind it—rather gothic.''

Tartly his mother said, ''I suppose you will tell me sometime today what this all means?''

''Can you not guess? Dolph, the carriage, the luggage, the two young ladies?''

Lady Margaret's eyes widened. ''You do not mean . . . Robert, tell me you do not mean an elopement?''

''Precisely.''

''And the lady involved?''

''The important lady was Miss Standish. No, no, it was not her luggage being roped to the roof, although now that I think about it, there was a question of one of the bandboxes having been borrowed from her without her permission. She represented in fact the only element of sanity to be seen. She was preventing the happy pair from pursuing their intentions.''

He fell silent, reliving the moment when he had first seen her standing defiantly before him, her eyes blazing, and he recognized—although perhaps not at that moment—that fate had brought Fenella back to him.

''Perhaps I should be able to sustain suspense better,'' said Lady Margaret. ''Truly I have been cosseted beyond my deserts, for until now members of my family have been able to inform me from beginning to end without omitting the crux of their tales. Robert?''

The last word was spoken on a rising inflection. Robert interpreted his mother's mood as dangerous, and hastened to supply the element so far missing.

''The prospective bride was Charlotte Fletcher.''

For once Lady Margaret had nothing to say for several minutes. At length she said in a hollow voice, ''Was Dolph expecting to start at the very moment you arrived?''

''Well, no. The horses were not yet between the poles. It did seem to me that the stableboys were not springing to their tasks. And Flint was overjoyed to see me.''

She thought a moment. ''But you have not told me what part the governess played.''

''Miss Standish had driven over in a curricle to prevent

the elopement. I do not know how she heard of it, but she was making strong representations on the subject of impropriety and scandal to that abominable schoolgirl, who had hysterics upon my arrival.''

Surprisingly, Lady Margaret chuckled. ''Poor Robert!''

''You may well say so.''

''Was her mother informed?''

''That scatterbrain? No, nor was Sir Eustace. However, it is my understanding that Miss Standish does not have the governance of the nuptially minded miss. But you will understand how it was that I sent him away.''

She nodded. ''He came directly to me without a word of this. I suppose that was to be expected.''

''But I cannot keep him from this upcoming outing without revealing the reason. And I should not wish Fenella to incur criticism on this account.''

''No, I can see that. Miss Standish is no tale-bearer, and no doubt she had her reasons for remaining silent.''

''I can suggest one or two. Sir Eustace would come roaring over here to challenge Dolph to a duel, and my cousin would run him through. I don't particularly care for that kind of scandal. Most important, I should not like to see Fenella subjected to Mrs. Fletcher's hysterics.''

Lady Margaret shuddered. ''How any delicately nurtured female can abide that kind of household!''

He agreed. ''So although I cannot prevent Dolph from coming along, he cannot be allowed to take advantage of the situation.''

''You think he is still interested in that child?''

''I think he has a distinct regard for her fortune.''

''I suppose you mean I should turn watchdog!''

Mildly Robert said, ''I should not dream of commenting adversely on your conduct, ma'am.''

''But I brought him here!''

''You could not have known the whole of it.''

''I should have suspected. He was too eager to inform me that you were hanging out for Sophy Fletcher. Very well, I shall take responsibility for his conduct onto my conscience.''

Quizzically Robert said, "I don't suppose—"

"No, Robert," his mother said firmly, "I shall not alter Mrs. Fletcher's excursion plans. You must go, you know."

He grimaced. "At least it will be soon over."

But in truth he looked forward with elation to whatever time he could spend with Fenella, even if it must be in the middle of a cloud of eager witnesses.

16

"**S**uch kindness on the part of Lady Margaret," Sophy said to Fenella later that day. "She need not have proposed that the children go along to Nottingham. She insisted that you accompany us as well."

"I would rather not," said Fenella. "There is much to do to prepare lessons in advance for Emma."

Sophy frowned. "Lady Margaret was quite definite. Such an educational experience for Emma and Fanny. I am sure you will enjoy the excursion."

Fenella understood there was no appeal from Lady Margaret's expressed wish. Had it been Lord Wolver's wish that she join the party, she might have approached the journey in better spirits. She read Sophy's intentions clearly: Fenella would be shunted off with the children, out of the way. Although she was fond of Emma and Fanny, her cheeks burned at the implication she was not fit company for anyone outside the schoolroom.

And yet, this was the lot of governesses. She had best try once more, and this time with determination, to scale down her notions of her own worth!

"I must take Emma away from you tomorrow. I am going to town to Miss Tyson's. I think a new ribbon would be just the thing for my feathered bonnet."

"Perhaps I might go along?" said Fenella. "I should enjoy looking at Miss Tyson's store of finery."

"Of course you may go with me," agreed Sophy, "but I am persuaded you will not need to purchase anything. You have a very nice gray merino that will do excellently.''

Fenella had not given a great deal of thought to her apparel recently. It was astonishing how one could dress decently on a very small amount of money. She did not realize that it made little difference to anyone precisely what she wore, since she possessed a sense of elegance that could not be hidden.

She thought ruefully that she still had far too many moments when she forgot her calling and conducted herself as though she were still Miss Standish of Oakhurst. If she were not to be dismissed from position after position, she needed to remember her station.

But suddenly the very nice gray merino, admired by Sophy, was woefully inadequate in Fenella's eyes. She was too well-bred to compete with her employer, but she toyed with the notion of developing a megrim or the toothache to avoid traveling in company with Robert and Sophy. She had a very shrewd sense of the cause of her desire to avoid seeing him with Mrs. Fletcher. He was rumored—by Sir Eustace— to be about to offer marriage to Sophy. But as long as the betrothal had not been announced, Fenella felt she might enjoy his company, even though their meetings were out of sight beyond the orchard.

Fenella grasped what small pleasures she found, and for the moment she was willing to let the future bring her what unhappiness it would. But she was *not* willing to wear the gray merino!

Her cheeks burning again each time she recalled Sophy's set-down, she sat silently in a corner of the coach. Since she had no expenses, she still had all of her quarter's wages at her disposal.

The coach pulled up before Miss Tyson's door.

Miss Tyson was a tiny birdlike woman, a pair of scissors on a ribbon around her neck. She welcomed them somewhat apprehensively.

"I have come, Miss Tyson," said Sophy graciously, "to see how you go on. Our plans have changed, and we do not go to London as soon as we expected. But we shall still want the gowns finished before autumn."

Miss Tyson flushed. "I assure you I will have them finished before then." She gazed nearsightedly at Sophy. She seemed anxious for them to leave. "Was there something else, Mrs. Fletcher?"

"May we see what you have done? I was not quite sure the green brocade would be quite the thing for Charlotte, you know."

Miss Tyson was excessively embarrassed. "Well, you see . . . under the circumstances, I thought it best not to start."

"Not to start!"

Fenella had moved away from the hallway into the room at the left of the entrance, where Miss Tyson kept a store of feathers and ribbons, gloves and mitts, shawls and lace.

She let her gaze linger on the bright colors, gold and emerald and ruby, and on the paler shades, delicate as a butterfly's wing. How she wished she could have everything in sight!

At length her eyes fell on a shawl of sea-green wool, deeply fringed in black, and she knew she must have it. It was just the thing to brighten up the gray merino and yet not be gaudy. She hoped the price would fall within the amount she had in her purse. She turned back to the discussion which had escalated in volume, if not in courtesy.

"Circumstances? I cannot think what you mean. I informed you we should be going to London for the Season."

"Well, if I spoke out of turn, I'm sure I'm sorry for it. But if you did not see fit to inform me of your change of plans, then I cannot be blamed for listening to others."

"But, Mama," Emma interrupted, "we're not going to London. You said so!"

"Emma! Hold your tongue!"

The damage, however, had been done. The seamstress bore a strong resemblance to a cat with feathers still on its whiskers. Her information had, to her mind, been proven correct.

"I shall await your further orders," said Miss Tyson, pleasantly aware that if there were a wedding gown in the offing, as she had heard from two of the maids at Chantrey

Manor, she would see Mrs. Fletcher coming back a bit more humbly to the best seamstress within a hundred miles.

Sophy flounced out to the coach, her two daughters close behind her. Fenella lingered for a few moments, and when she emerged she carried a small parcel in her hand. No one noticed it, and she tucked it behind the carriage cushion.

They visited several shops in the village. Mrs. Fletcher gave her footman leave, and handed her parcels to Fenella. At last, since the packages were beginning to slide out of her grasp, she told Sophy she would take their purchases to the coach and return to her.

Before she reached the inn before which the coach stood, she saw Dolph Thorne in her way. She had not had occasion to speak to him since the thwarted elopement, and she was not certain of his attitude.

"Good afternoon, Miss Standish."

Very well, he was disposed to be civil. With an inner sigh of relief, she greeted him.

"I am just on my way to put these parcels in the coach. Mrs. Fletcher and the girls have shopped their way to the far end of the street!"

"Then I am fortunate in finding you alone, even though briefly."

"Alone? I do not understand you."

"May I walk with you to your vehicle? Let me carry your parcels for you."

He turned and walked with her the few steps to the coach. After he had stowed his burden within, he turned to her. "I wonder if you can let bygones be bygones, Miss Standish?"

"There is no need to ask for my silence, Mr. Thorne. I fancy Charlotte has learned a lesson, and I see no need for tale-bearing."

"I commend you for your discretion."

"I have not told Sir Eustace about the elopement." A shadow passed over his features, and somehow she was uneasy for a moment. "I think it best to be perfectly frank with you, Mr. Thorne. I make no promises to you for the future. I told Charlotte that were an incident of that kind to happen again, my own duty would be plain."

His face hardened, and she saw lines that made him appear ten years older than he was. "Let sleeping dogs lie, Miss Standish," he said softly, "or you might stir up more trouble than you can handle."

Dolph realized he had made a mistake. She thought he referred to that foiled elopement. Well, let her think that was his meaning. He would, however, keep close watch on her, and if she twigged him on that subject that he wished to remain buried, he knew what to do about it.

She watched him as he strode down the street. She was not sure what she had just heard. It had sounded remarkably like a threat. But why would he threaten her? She must have misunderstood him.

Just the same, she felt unsettled. He had gone away swiftly, in the direction in which he might already have found the Fletchers. She was unwilling to return to Sophy, lest she meet Dolph again.

She was a few doors away from the vicarage gate. She recalled that Mrs. Roseacre had promised Sophy a recipe for raspberry trifle, and she turned in that direction.

Too late she saw Lord Wolver approaching from the other direction. There was no help for it. She met him just at the gate.

"Good afternoon, Miss Standish! Have you come to town alone?"

"No," she reassured him. "Mrs. Fletcher is at the other end of the street."

"I suppose you are bound to accompany her back to Chantrey Manor? If not, I hope I may carry you there myself." He added carefully, "In my curricle. Perfectly proper."

In spite of herself, she chuckled. "Perfectly proper" was not the term to be used for their meeting beyond the orchard!

"I must decline," she said regretfully. "Mrs. Fletcher expects me to join her in her shopping within a few moments. I see now there is not sufficient time to call on Mrs. Roseacre. I defer to your business at the vicarage."

"I have just learned," he explained, "that I have the gift

of this living, and I wish to assure Mr. Roseacre that he will not be put upon the parish.''

''How thoughtful!''

''Not at all. If I am to meet him in company, as I assume I shall two days hence, we shall all be more comfortable if this is settled.''

The vicar himself joined them at the gate. He had overheard only Robert's last few words, and greeted his patron with a broad smile.

''Ah, my lord, come to have the banns put up?''

Then it was true! Fenella felt warmth rise from her throat into her face. She prayed Wolver had not seen her telltale blush.

But Robert was too surprised to notice. ''Banns? Why should I ask for banns?''

Jollying me, thought the vicar. Well, I can give as good as I get! ''Seeing your intentions so well-known, my lord, it's understandable that I should like the privilege of seeing one of my parishioners find a happy life.''

''I assure you,'' said Robert, bewildered, ''that I am perfectly happy already.''

''Ah, the felicity of a ready-made family must outrank any happiness claimed by the single life.''

Too late, the vicar noted that unsmiling face of his patron. He should not have mentioned what everybody in town knew—that Lord Wolver spent much of his time in Mrs. Fletcher's drawing-room. His mother had been sent for, as well, and Mr. Roseacre's dreams portrayed himself in full canonicals officiating at what would be the wedding of the century in this parish.

Too eager, too eager! It might, judging from the grim visage of the prospective bridegroom, even cost him his living!

Lord Wolver was rarely angry. However, the tight rein he kept on his temper was sorely strained at this moment.

''I came to call on you,'' he said to the vicar, ''on business, not mine, but your own. I shall join you presently.''

''I—'' Whatever apology Mr. Roseacre had in mind fled

under the gaze of the unyielding blue eyes. He followed suit, retreating speedily to the vicarage door.

Fenella saw her comfortable friendship—it could no longer be more!—in shards around her feet. She must think of graceful words to say to make an orderly departure, but she could not speak.

Robert watched her for a moment. All he could see was the top of her plain round bonnet, but a tremor in her hand told him she was distressed far beyond the ordinary. On a light note he said, "I may change my mind on this gossipy vicar."

She looked up quickly. "Oh, but where would he go if you cast him out?"

"I know what it is," he said gently, "to be cast out without hope."

She reddened. He regretted the words even as they left his lips.

He had not the slightest intention at any time of being more than civil to Mrs. Fletcher. Indeed he found her an intolerable obstacle between him and Fenella. But till this moment he had dwelt in false security, being unacquainted with the power of village rumor.

Now this clergyman had informed him that he was far wide of the mark. But how could one say to a lady, "I do not wish to marry you," when the subject had never come up between them?

He answered Fenella's question. "I have a suggestion as to where he should go, but I believe it is not proper to mention it to a clergyman."

Fenella's lips twitched. Why did he always make her laugh?

She was enchanting, thought Robert, but this meddling vicar must be dealt with at once. He bowed over her hand and sternly repressed his instinct to watch her down the street.

When at last the Fletcher coach trundled toward home, Emma ventured, "If we are not going to London, then I do not need to study French."

Her mother disagreed. "We will go to London, but not quite yet."

Fenella, retrieving the parcel holding her shawl, lapsed into reverie. Her heart had bounced, she recalled, at the sight of Robert approaching her. She had been uncomfortable with him when first they met again, remembering all that had passed between them. Now she was more at ease with him, at least until the vicar had interrupted them.

But the meeting at the vicarage gate had told her truths she had not wanted to know. She was more aware than ever that she entertained a deepening passion for Robert, now, when it was too late.

She could not credit Robert and Sophy as a betrothed couple! If the town believed that Sophy was about to marry him, then she, Fenella, was a fool and had not seen what everyone else had noticed.

She had never run from her troubles before, but then, she had never been so unsettled before, swinging this way and that, torn by her own desires and what she feared was the truth.

By the time the coach drew up before the entrance to Chantrey Manor, she had come to the conclusion that Robert had not looked happy as the vicar had relayed the rumors, and she hoped it was not merely because of his indiscretion.

Perhaps she should wait until Robert himself told her he loved Sophy!

17

The destination of Sophy Fletcher's expedition designed to amuse Lady Margaret had changed once again. Upon Lord Wolver's discovery that a journey as far as the famous statue of Robin Hood would be above sixteen miles, he promptly seized his opportunity.

"Far too arduous!" he informed her. "I shall not allow you to become overly tired."

Lady Margaret was finding her son a much more interesting creature these days than when he was adolescent. More interesting, yes, but no less transparent. What was in the man's head now?

"Nonsense! It was above thirty miles from Thorne Abbey to Stockton Priory, and I endured it perfectly well."

"This is different, you must agree. You will be expected to get out of the carriage and walk to view the church and the Major Oak and the cathedral. No, no, it is too much."

"I confess I should be glad enough to stay home, but I cannot avoid the trip on such a feeble excuse."

Robert caught the twinkle in his mother's eye, and knew she was not deceived by his arguments. He teased her, "You haven't looked the thing lately—"

"I am in my best looks, and you know it." She studied him through narrowed eyelids. "You don't want to be seen in company with the Fletcher woman."

Robert inclined his head.

"But, Robert, you cannot simply decline such an invitation. The party is made up. You will offend too many people.

Only think: the squire, Lady Clavering, Dolly, the children, the vicar and his wife—''

Savagely he snarled, ''Don't mention Roseacre to me!''

''I need not, if you do not like it. But there are others to whom one cannot be rude.''

''It is not just a matter of not wishing to be seen even in company with that woman. I simply dare not.''

Casting wildly about in her mind for an explanation of his remark, she wondered whether he was so overcome with passion that he might make advances to Sophy under the vicar's nose. No, her common sense said, that cannot be.

''Best tell me,'' she told him, ''or I shall imagine all sorts of bizarre things.''

''Very well. I went down to reassure Roseacre that he might be confirmed in his living. He had the audacity to confront me and ask whether I had come to put up the banns. For an upcoming wedding. And, I must tell you, one that would provide me with a ready-made family!''

''Good God,'' Lady Margaret said with feeling. ''Has he run mad?''

''No, just gossipy. A turn he will regret, I promise you.''

''He could not mean—''

''But he did. I took him inside the vicarage and tried to squeeze the truth out of him. I think I had some success. It seems that he and the entire town are expecting daily to hear that I have offered for Sophy Fletcher.''

''Anybody blind in one eye could see the falsity in that. Who is spreading this rumor, Robert? The lady herself?''

''As far as I can tell, word has come from the Chantrey Manor servants. But their credibility can be judged by the vicar's conviction.''

''Indeed yes. But, Robert, you cannot simply ignore the whole!''

''What else can I do? To deny this rumor publicly . . .'' He threw up his hands in a gesture of helplessness.

After a few moments, Lady Margaret asked delicately, ''And Fenella?''

He groaned. ''She was standing beside me. And heard the whole of it.''

"And the vicar blurted it all out? The man's mad. I recommend you have him put away. Let me think a moment." After a short silence she inquired, "Is there a local point of interest nearer at hand than Robin Hood?"

"Let me ask Napier."

Summoned, the butler mentioned a robber's cave in the side of a hill, a ruin of an old abbey, a lake said to be haunted by a monk carrying his head in the crook of his left arm, and a church with a Saxon wall still standing.

After he had been dismissed, Lady Margaret said, "I believe one of these will do. Certainly not the haunted lake, but the Saxon wall perhaps. We can all travel to that spot for our day's excursion. I can keep Fenella by me for the entire day on such a short excursion, and you may dance attendance on us if you please . . ."

He grinned. "That won't be difficult!"

"And do stay away from the widow!"

"I never thought I would ask my mother to pay court for me."

His mother answered dryly, "Nor should I, save that I like Fenella so much."

Hopefully he asked, "Perhaps I need not go at all?"

"You must not be discourteous to the squire and his lady, nor to my dear Dolly." In an altered tone she asked, "Have you spoken to Fenella?"

"Not in the way you mean, ma'am. I have contrived to see her away from the house, and I think she may return my regard. Unless the vicar's idiocy has put a spoke in my wheel!"

The day of the expedition dawned clear and mild, to Sophy's relief. At first Lady Margaret had mentioned Scarborough, but as soon as Sophy planned an outing in that direction, Lady Margaret changed her mind.

Robin Hood! Who would go miles to see a statue or a church? Clearly Lady Margaret would not, for after Sophy's cook had threatened to leave rather than prepare an *al fresco* luncheon for twenty persons including coachmen and grooms (and the order had been withdrawn), word came from the

Priory that the journey was deemed too far and a substitute objective was proposed. It was almost as though Lady Margaret were putting difficulties in her way for a reason.

Sophy had been flattered by Lord Wolver's first visit to Chantrey Manor.

He had seemingly had no reason to return, as he did several days that next week, and yet he had. At first, Sophy had no idea of making a change in her life, but Wolver's attentions fanned a small ember that she thought had died long ago.

Truthfully, Wolver had said nothing to her that could not be shouted from the rooftops. But there was the inescapable fact that he had called frequently at Chantrey Manor, that he lingered in the vicinity longer than anyone expected him to, and that only a couple of days after he had first met her, his mother had arrived.

Sophy's hopes rested on the slightest of foundations, yet they grew apace, fed on dislike of Sir Eustace, boredom with her lot, and a longing for the romance that existed in books but had been no part of her husband's character.

Sophy awoke with a headache, having spent the better part of the night in troubling dreams. She had no thought, however, of staying at home, for Lord Wolver had promised to make one of the party, and she would spend the day with him were she to die the next week of a chill.

The company assembled at Chantrey Manor. Robert was driving a curricle and pair, two of the other gentlemen were riding, and Lady Margaret carried Lady Clavering, Mrs. Roseacre, and Dolly Pruitt in her spacious carriage. Sophy's carriage held herself and her daughters, and Fenella.

The party was about to depart. The first carriage, Lady Margaret's, was already starting down the drive, escorted by Dolph and Mr. Pruitt riding alongside, when one of the inhabitants of Chantrey Manor took exception to the arrangements.

Muggins escaped from the tight grasp of the underfootman and dashed in front of Sophy's coach, barking ferociously at the lead horses. The left wheeler, young and rather undisciplined, was not certain of the nature of the commotion, but he knew he did not like it. He plunged in the traces, and it took the combined efforts of two grooms to quiet him.

Fenella leaned from the coach window. "Muggins! You naughty dog! Come here at once!"

Muggins, hearing the beloved voice, galloped back to give his mistress a wheedling look and wag a beguiling tail. Fenella told him, "Now be a good boy and let Beccles take you to the stables. You will like that." Her tone, however, was not in the least intimidating, and Muggins gave signs of racing back to prevent the coach from moving, if need be.

Robert, holding his horses steady, watched the scene with carefully hidden amusement. He was aware that discussion was taking place inside the coach and he surmised correctly that Mrs. Fletcher was adamantly refusing to allow the dog to travel with her. It was equally clear that the dog would be restrained only with major force. He summoned one of the grooms and handed his reins over.

Walking to the coach, he interrupted Sophy. "May I suggest that, since the dog seems determined to come along, I take him in the curricle? I think we must delay no longer, for my mother's coach is long out of sight."

"Very well," said Sophy grudgingly. "But someone must go with you to hold the beast. My head aches, and I should be glad of the open air."

Swiftly sidestepping the abyss he saw opening before him, he said pleasantly, "I should think the dog might behave better were Miss Standish to come. He seems to have a great partiality for her."

Sophy rested her head on the cushions and waved Fenella to obey. "Why you ever let that dog loose, I cannot think."

Fenella reluctantly left the carriage. Trembling on her lips was a denial that she had loosed the dog, as well as a refusal to ride with Lord Wolver.

But Robert had already helped her to the ground and was guiding her toward his vehicle. "A very handsome shawl, Miss Standish," he said for the benefit of the footman holding Muggins and the groom at the head of his horses.

He handed her up to the seat. The groom handed the wriggling dog to her and swung up behind.

She scarcely acknowledged Robert's compliment, and they were down the drive and turning to follow the others before he dared to speak again.

"I must be gateful to Muggins."

"Grateful? He should be whipped!" But her hand gently stroked the small body on her lap.

"I did not at first see any means to persuade you to ride with me, but the dog came to my rescue."

She stiffened. She too had spent a sleepless night. She knew, as she had known from the first, that Lord Wolver was several cuts above her now. It was excessively ill-bred to meet him in the shrubbery—like a lovestick dairymaid— and even more foolish to believe that she did no harm to anyone to indulge in his company for an hour or two. The harm she had done was devastating, and it was done to herself.

Robert was dismayed. The vicar's ill-timed gossip had done a good deal of damage, and Robert set himself to retrieving his credit with her as he could.

"You are very silent," he said after they had driven a mile. "Your head aches also?"

"You must agree," she said tartly, "that this is most improper."

"Improper? With my groom up in back? Besides, Muggins will certainly protect you from any untoward advances on my part."

Muggins, feeling the hand that had been stroking him suddenly become rigid, took exception and uttered an admonitory growl at Robert.

"You see I am right."

She could find no words to express her feelings. She was elated over having him next to her, the clean smell of soap that was so much a part of him and was one of her clearest memories of him. But she was wrong to be with him, very wrong to entertain the thoughts that came unbidden to her. She had refused him once, and masculine pride must avoid another rejection, must it not?

If they could only drive on so, until they reached the end of the world!

"That stupid Roseacre is at the bottom of your sulks," said Robert in an even voice. "I wish he had at least held his tongue."

"I do not blame you," she said, "for being angry at his premature disclosure. How his ill-timed congratulations must have galled you!"

Robert was moved to explode, "Do you think for a moment . . . ?" He recalled the groom riding at the back, and lowered his voice. "Can you possibly think that I have the slightest interest in such a silly woman?"

Fenella found it hard to breathe. Had she been wrong? Was it possible he would not offer for her employer? "Everybody thinks so."

"Why in God's name should they?"

"Because you have called so often at Chantrey Manor, and stayed in the vicinity far longer than you gave out at the start."

"Everybody. Including you?"

When she finally answered, she spoke in such a low voice that he strained to hear her. He admitted that even so, her remarks were incoherent. "Well, I did think so, and everybody said so, and the vicar expected—"

"And the vicar is a damned fool!" He looked back at the groom, and groaned in frustration. "I shall hope to persuade you otherwise, my dear girl. But at a more approriate time and place!"

Fenella rode the rest of the way in a kind of euphoria. Perhaps *they* were all wrong! Perhaps he did find her more than attractive! Perhaps . . . But *that* far she dared not imagine.

The excursion drew at last toward its close. Lady Margaret had been true to her pledge to her son, and had devoted the afternoon to keeping Fenella by her side. She found the girl as delightful as her mother, and now she longed ardently for Robert's suit to prosper, for her own sake as well as his.

Luncheon had been obtained at a country inn, after which the entire entourage had traveled a mile beyond, where, on a small grassy knoll rising from the center of a beech wood, stood half a church wall. The stones that had once been a part of the structure now lay in disarray down the slope, and unnamed birds soared high above in the cloudless sky.

Having looked their full at the church, which in some persons required less than a moment, the members of the party separated. Sophy caught Fenella's arm and told her, "I really do not feel well, Fenella. I am so cold."

Truly, Sophy was looking very sickly, and her hand in Fenella's was icy. "Let me help you to a place where you may sit in the sun. The heat will be good for you. Here, wrap this around your shoulders," said Fenella, bravely sacrificing her new green shawl that Lord Wolver had admired.

After she found a suitable stump at the edge of the wood and settled Sophy on it, leaning against the young tree that had grown from the stump probably fifty years before, she moved away.

The woods were delightful in their first green, and Fenella enjoyed being left to her own devices. She was agreeably pleased that Sophy had been amenable enough not to protest the makeshift seat on the stump. A little breeze sprang up, and Fenella felt the lack of her shawl. Her gray merino may have been suitable, according to Sophy, but it was not quite warm enough.

Fenella walked briskly along the edge of the wood. Although she did not admit it to herself, she hoped every moment for a sight of Lord Wolver. However, she first came upon the forlorn figure of Charlotte standing alone next to the light gray trunk of a giant beech.

When Fenella approached, she noted the girl's red nose and swollen eyes, still brimming with tears. Also, and more distressing, she caught sight of a red mark on her cheek, clearly the shape of a palm. So, Dolph had hit her!

Fenella placed her arm around Charlotte's shoulders. "Tell me, what happened?"

With some difficulty, Fenella elicited the cause of Charlotte's unhappiness. "I had to send him away," she told Fenella. "He wanted me to run away again, but I said I was afraid of my grandfather."

Startled, Fenella asked, "Did you tell Sir Eustace about that first time?"

"Oh, no, I couldn't! And I didn't mean that I was precisely afraid either. I only meant that Grandfather would not like it if I ran away. I had not thought much about it the other time, but, Fenella, Dolph was so angry!"

"I am not surprised. But why did he think that striking you would change your mind? Your grandfather would like your marriage even less if he knew."

Charlotte was calmer now. "Where were you just now, Fenella? I mean, just before you found me?"

"Your mother was not well, and I was with her. I think we had best start as soon as possible for Chantrey Manor. She should be lying on her bed. Why does it matter where I was?"

"Because Dolph said you were too nosy, and blamed you for interfering. I wondered if you were listening to us then. But if you were with Mother, then that's all right."

It might be all right with Charlotte, thought Fenella wryly, but it was far from pleasing to Fenella to be accused, as it were, of eavesdropping on a private conversation.

If that were what Charlotte thought of her, no wonder Fenella could not instruct her on the ways of proper society!

18

Fenella sent Charlotte back to the coach.

"Please tell your mother I am trying to find the others to send them back to the vehicles. Why they all had to scatter, I cannot see!"

She had no idea of the direction in which Lord Wolver had gone, nor his mother. After Fenella had left her, Lady Margaret had shown a surprising turn of speed when it was a question of ridding herself of the company of Mrs. Roseacre and the squire's wife, and even of Dolly. Lady Margaret did not suffer fools gladly, and it took the greatest effort on her part to remain civil.

Fenella's search was not thorough. She was convinced that the older ladies would soon tire and return unbidden to the carriages. She would give herself a few more moments of blessed quiet before she turned back herself.

She remembered that most of England had once been covered with forest, and in places patches of woodlands survived. There were glades in it, open stretches of gorse, and great oak and beech trees. In just such a forest as this, Robin Hood had lived.

Fantasies of Robin Hood, however, failed to capture her interest for long. More immediate to her mind's eye were the features of Lord Wolver. He had certainly eased her mind about his interest in Sophy Fletcher, and Fenella felt herself free to think about him, to meet him privately at the back of the orchard, even to wonder whether what was done could be undone.

She stopped short. The rustling of last year's leaves on the floor of the woodland ceased with her steps, and a great quiet fell on her. Far away she could hear some indistinguished high sounds, but they did not disturb her.

Her turmoil was within herself. She knew she had changed during the three years since she had seen Robert. But how much had he altered in the interval? It was true that recently they had talked of many things, and she had found his judgments on various topics to her taste. But he was also now an experienced gallant, the object of many a matrimonial lure since he had inherited title and wealth.

She felt the sand shifting beneath her feet, so to speak. In a moment she realized that truly the ground was giving way, and she cried out as she fell to her knees.

The leaves were rustling still, and she had a vision of a wild creature, probably a maddened boar, approaching with vicious intent. Surprisingly, a voice spoke above her.

"Are you hurt?" demanded Lord Wolver in a voice so concerned that she felt tears spring to her eyes.

How awkward to be found sprawled on a forest floor, skirt rucked up, and, she discovered as she struggled to sit up, a wet leaf plastered to her cheek!

He knelt beside her. "Any bones broken? You must be shaken up. Do not try to rise just yet."

His arm went around her shoulders and pulled her close. Without thought her head dropped to his shoulder. She realized she was trembling, but not from the fall, which had truly been trivial. She tested her ankles. "I believe I can walk, sir. There is no harm done, save to my *amour-propre*."

"And why should that have suffered? A small animal tunnel, doubtless, and no one could have avoided it."

He took her wrist, obviously the one she had fallen on, displaying small pieces of leaf and forest debris, with his free hand and flexed it. She felt warmth creeping over her body, and knew her face was reddening.

"Lord Wolver . . ." she protested faintly.

"My name, as you well know, is Robert."

"Oh, I cannot!"

"Cannot? Will you tell me precisely what you cannot? Call me Robert? Rise to your feet if I help you? Wear that bonnet again?"

His tone was teasing, and there was no reason why she should feel so wretched. But she did not wish him to see how much his gentle caressing hand on her wrist had overset her. Determined to ignore what she could not accept, she answered crisply, "I do think I can stand."

He eyed her quizzically. He did not seem to regard the situation as unusual. He had never before sat on a bed of leaves in a wood holding a very attractive lady in his arms, but he found it pleasant, and as long as there seemed to be no physical damage to the lady, he was in no hurry to make a change.

"You do not understand," she said. "Suppose someone were to come!"

"I should stuff him down the nearest badger hole," he said promptly. But he recognized the force of her protest and withdrew his arm. On his feet, he reached his hand to help her up. He did not relinquish her hand, once she was standing. She knew herself unhurt, with no need for his support, but she did not pull her hand away.

"How is it," he asked, "that you are alone here?"

"I was looking for the rest of our party," she told him. "It is time to return to the Manor, and now I cannot find Muggins."

"Listen!"

Far and away she heard again the high sounds, and now she recognized them as Muggins' distinctive yelps. They followed the sound until they came upon him, digging vigorously at the base of an ancient tree, more hollow than solid.

His busy tail was all she could see at the start, but when she called his name, he backed out and whined before he plunged to his task again. He was determined to rout out some small unseen creature, which was protesting in little muffled cries.

When Lord Wolver spoke to him, however, he looked

startled, but bowed to authority and reluctantly abandoned his prey. Fenella picked him up, and they retraced their steps to the edge of the wood.

She had supposed that at least Sophy's carriage would have started on its way back to the Manor, since Sophy had indeed seemed ill and would be longing for her bed. But the Fletcher carriage stood as it had been.

There appeared to be as well an inordinate amount of coming and going of people. Mrs. Roseacre was bending over something on the ground, and Lady Clavering was sobbing loudly, but both ladies took time to examine without favor the approaching pair. Fenella instinctively glanced at Lady Margaret, standing a little aside, and was reassured by her smile.

The center of attention was Sophy, lying partly on the ground, her upper body supported by Mrs. Pruitt. Fenella's shawl was wrapped untidily around her employer's head, apparently to ward off a draft. Sophy was subject to the earache, so she often said.

Lady Margaret caught her son's eye. "You must hear what has happened," she said. "Perhaps we should draw a little apart, so as not to distress the lady."

Obediently they followed her out of earshot of the others. Instead of explaining, however, she asked Fenella, "When did you give that handsome shawl to Mrs. Fletcher?"

"Only a short time ago. She said she was chilled, so I wrapped her in it and found a place for her to sit. What has happened?"

"She was apparently struck from behind only a few moments ago. Lady Clavering came back to the carriage and found her nearby on the ground, in a faint."

Lady Clavering could be heard lamenting, "I should never have gone away. I thought she was napping in the coach. I never dreamed . . . If I had stayed with her . . ."

Robert exclaimed testily, "Is this entire county peopled with fools? Had she been nearby, she would have stood a good chance of being struck herself."

"I cannot think it was a robber, for only a lackwit would

think there was gold in a group on a picnic! And the blow was not severe.''

Puzzled, Fenella inquired, ''I do not precisely know what has happened. Mrs. Fletcher was struck from behind, I think you said? By whom? And with what? Did a tree limb drop?''

''A tree limb may have been the weapon,'' said Lady Margaret, ''but the gentlemen seem to think it was wielded by a human hand. Mrs. Fletcher had apparently folded the shawl around her head, and that fact saved her from serious injury.''

Catching sight of his mother's expression, Robert laughed slightly. ''No, much as I dislike the woman, I did not strike that blow! Miss Standish will bear witness that I was with her.'' Smiling, he added, ''Searching for the dog.''

Fenella looked troubled. ''That is true, ma'am.'' How indiscreet she had been! The two of them, alone in the forest, as innocent as could be, and yet the appearance of it was of near-depravity! Biting her lip, she recalled her duty. ''I should go to Charlotte and Emma. They must be worried.''

Lady Margaret watched her go before she turned to her son. ''Robert, what on earth could you be thinking of? Do you not know how gossip runs wild in this neighborhood?''

''I trust my future actions will carry off whatever scandal those nimble-tongued women can devise.'' In answer to the question in her eyes, he responded, ''No, I have not yet offered. But I will, and soon. She is harried beyond endurance by that family, and I have not found the right moment. But I confess to you that I do not like it that the victim was wearing that distinctive shawl when she was struck.''

Fenella was worried as well. There was no reason whatever for Sophy to be injured by another. But several questions jostled each other in her head. She knew that Robert had been with her, supposing the attack to have come only a short time before. But there was violence in young Dolph, she knew.

He had seemed to threaten her that day in town, and she had not promised to hold her tongue in the future. But would he resort to force? She had a strong desire to lay the problem before Lord Wolver, but Dolph was his kin, and she shrank from seeming to criticize him.

She found the girls, who were solemn and frightened, and reassured them. "I am told your mother will be fine. She was not hurt seriously, and although she will have the headache for some days, she will suffer no lasting damage." She hoped her information was correct.

Much subdued, the party gathered itself to return home. The girls were squeezed into Lady Margaret's coach so that Sophy could lie on the seat of her own carriage. Fenella was to accompany the victim.

As she was about to climb into the coach, Lord Wolver came to speak to her. "My mother and I," he said distinctly for the benefit of any eavesdroppers, "will call tomorrow to see how Mrs. Fletcher goes on." His tone was properly civil, but his eyes told Fenella a different story. She warmed under his glance.

He stretched his hand out to help her into the coach, at which time everyone within some distance became aware that the small dog took exception to his lady leaving him behind.

"Oh, dear," said Fenella, "whatever shall I do with him? Mrs. Fletcher takes great exception to dogs."

"I shall relieve you of him," said Robert, "and bring him back to you tomorrow."

Fenella climbed up and the door was closed. Muggins was ready to make a great scene, Robert suspected, remembering the ploy by which he had come on this jaunt at the start. But Muggins, hearing a word in a voice that he had heard only shortly before and recognized as one that it did not do to ignore, followed his temporary master to his curricle and bounded up onto the seat. At least, his canine thoughts went, he would not be totally abandoned!

Muggins was not the only creature who feared abandonment. In Lady Margaret's coach, Charlotte gave way to excessive gloom. The ladies believed she was concerned about her mother, and made several reassuring statements, but upon receiving no answer from her, desisted.

Charlotte's thoughts ran along quite another line. She loved

Dolph, at least she supposed she did, since she had almost run away with him. Just think, if Fenella had not stopped them and Lord Wolver had not come upon them in time, she would now be Mrs. Dolph Thorne and living someplace far removed from here.

For the first time, she could not look upon that future with unrelieved optimism. Dolph had sworn he wanted to marry her. Charlotte was not particularly intelligent, but she did know that it was customary for a suitor to approach the head of the family for permission to pay his addresses. The elopement, of course, was such a romantic idea that the notion of returning from Scotland already married, and astonishing her family, was irresistible.

Now, however, their secret attachment was no longer secret. Dolph's cousin knew, Fenella knew, and most likely Emma knew, for someone had informed Fenella, and who could that be but prying Emma? Charlotte knew full well that she would be watched closely to prevent another such escapade, and she had told Dolph that Fenella would certainly inform Sir Eustace of any untoward incident. He had really frightened her then, cursing Fenella for her ill-timed interference.

Dolph had insisted on surrounding their trysts—which continued, although Fenella was not aware of it—with great secrecy. She thought, of course, he wished to foil Fenella's discovery of their most improper meetings. But Charlotte could not understand why, if he did love her, he did not seek to marry her in the approved manner. When she had asked him that very question this afternoon, he had flown into a fury and slapped her hard, and left her.

He had never before been so unfeeling. It must be her own fault for questioning him. She must be more careful in the future, studying how not to bring that temper to the surface.

In her inexperienced mind, she believed she could make changes in herself, learn to do things the way he wanted, and then he would love her more.

This was what she wanted above all things. Wasn't it?

19

If Sophy's injury were not a threat to her life, no one in Chantrey Manor was allowed to think so. Upon arrival home, she had to be helped, nearly fainting, into the house and carried upstairs.

Fenella had been privileged to look at the wound, and found it shallow and scarcely bleeding. It was her opinion that by far the major part of Sophy's weakness on arriving home was a queasiness caused by the action of the coach.

But of course the doctor who had taken care of the Fletchers for a generation was summoned, and pronounced her to be on the mend already. "No need to cosset yourself, Mrs. Fletcher," he told her. "Best get on your feet as soon as you can."

His advice was unwelcome, and Sophy termed it quackery. "I fear the man is growing senile!" she exclaimed, then proceeded to stay in her bed and brood over her wrongs.

She had endured a trying few weeks, she reflected. The new heir to Stockton Priory had been anticipated, since Lord Wolver's young cousin explained that he had been sent ahead to make all ready for the earl's arrival.

Social life in the valley was hardly strenuous, and any newcomer was joyfully welcomed, especially one of title. To her surprise, Lord Wolver had called at once. She had been greatly flattered, even though each time he was not inclined to linger more than the expected fifteen minutes. Such excellent breeding, said Sophy; he knows exactly how to go on.

Almost imperceptibly the idea crept upon her that Lord Wolver could be induced to take an interest in her. Certainly he did not come to see Sir Eustace particularly, for as often as not that gentleman was not present to greet the visitor. Sophy introduced Charlotte to him, but she could not stretch her imagination to encompass the notion that Lord Wolver was interested in her elder daughter.

Then why did he come several times a week? Certainly he was paying distinguished attention to Chantrey Manor, and, therefore, since no one else seemed to be an attraction to him, she concluded that he came to call on her.

Sophy had never been at home in the larger social circles of England. She had had a month in London during the Season, and had been so devastated by homesickness that her mother carried her away in disgust. Her marriage to Sir Eustace's son had followed shortly afterward, and upon his death she had removed to Chantrey Manor and never traveled far from it.

Out of touch with London news, she was ignorant of the wide swath Robert Thorne had cut in London after he had returned from a dashing military career. Therefore, she was not aware that, even before inheriting his great-uncle's title and wealth, he was considered an enormous catch, and an exceptionally wily one, who continued to slip away from the most tempting bait dangled before him.

Therefore, noting that the earl lingered at his manor far longer than anticipated, and remarking that her competition was nonexistent, she could be excused for believing herself to be the object of Lord Wolver's attention.

In this belief she was at first encouraged by her father-in-law, who saw in Wolver a rescuer of a kind not to be ignored. If Sophy became a countess, she could go to London with his good wishes, provided she took her silly daughters with her and allowed his house to return to the peace and quiet he demanded.

He wouldn't miss any of them, save perhaps for the governess woman, Fenella. A fine-looking woman, and he might even offer for her himself when his daughter-in-law left.

He greeted Lord Wolver when he called, as promised, the next day after the ill-fated outing.

"Came to see Sophy, did you?" said Sir Eustace jovially. "Can't do it. She's out of it!"

"Good God!" said Robert, startled. "I was told by the ladies that the wound was superficial. I did not expect her to take any harm from it."

"Doctor says she's good as cured, but she complains of the headache, and won't have any but the governess tending her."

Seeing his hope of being alone with Fenella vanishing down the wind, Robert said all the proper things concerning the return to health of the invalid, and made ready to leave. He stepped into the hall, followed by Sir Eustace, and encountered the butler. The odd expression on that servant's features arrested Robert in his tracks. Following the direction of the butler's expressive gaze, he saw the last thing in the world he wanted to see.

Sophy had risen from her sickbed upon hearing Wolver's curricle wheels, and she was descending the stairs at the moment that Robert emerged from the salon. A muscle twitched at the corner of Robert's mouth, but with great restraint he bowed to her and said, "I trust I see you better, ma'am?"

"You came!" she exclaimed with fervor.

Sir Eustace, eyeing Lord Wolver narrowly, detected not the slightest tremor of concern in his voice. Nor, to be truthful at last, did Sir Eustace really expect Wolver to come up to the mark. All he had told himself was rubbish, and Sophy had wind in her head, as he had always claimed.

Besides, the governess woman had come down the stairs hurriedly behind Sophy, and Sir Eustace, blustering and self-centered and rough as a farmhand, was no fool. He caught the fleeting warmth in the earl's eyes as he caught sight of Fenella, and suddenly he understood all.

It was as though scales fell from his eyes. What a mull his silly daughter-in-law had made of it! His own part in kindling Sophy's foolish expectations was conveniently, and permanently, forgotten.

Lord Wolver bowed, keeping his distance from Sophy, and in moments had left the house. The housekeeper was summoned to assist Fenella in getting Sophy up the stairs again, and Sir Eustace, his head full of conflicting and thought-provoking notions, retreated to the library and called for whiskey.

Fenella had caught the intimate glance that Robert meant for her, and dangled between hope and despair about its meaning. She could no longer think that Robert was enamored of Sophy Fletcher, but that conviction did not lead directly to the conclusion she longed for.

She wished she could see him now, even for a moment, to feel her hand engulfed in his, to see that smile that changed his expression so delightfully.

Sophy kept her close at hand, not allowing her time enough away from her even to step outside the house, and picking up a shawl and hurrying on light feet to the walk beyond the orchard was out of the question. Besides, she was still haunted by the thought that had she kept her shawl, and found Sophy some other wrap against the chill, she herself might now be laid low. She would not have folded the shawl around her head, so the blow would have fallen with much more severity. She did not want to think about it.

A sennight after the unhappy outing, Sir Eustace made a morning visit to Sophy in her sitting room. She had recovered so far as to don a dressing-gown and move from her bed to a chair near the fire. Sir Eustace signaled to Fenella to leave, and closed the door behind her. She never knew what was said in that interview, but after lunch that day Sophy said in a casual manner, "I fear I have been keeping you much inside. I am so sorry. I do not wish you to undermine your health with caring for me."

Fenella murmured something.

"I have an excellent idea!" Sophy continued. "I am reminded of that silver rose I ordered from Miss Tyson. Do you recall it?"

"I believe it was to be fastened to the deep blue India muslin," agreed Fenella.

"Exactly. I dread to recall my last meeting with Miss

Tyson. Do you think she might be so angry that she would not keep the rose for me?''

Fenella could not reassure her, for in fact she thought Miss Tyson might well dispose of the rose as well as the fabrics set aside for the ladies at Chantrey Manor, and consider them well-served. At length, Sophy charged her with obtaining the silver rose and bringing it to lodge in safety in Sophy's own hands. Other errands were mentioned, and in early afternoon Fenella set out for Shackleton in the curricle, the groom on the seat beside her.

It felt good to have the reins of a lively pair in her hand again. She glanced at the sky. This was not the day she would have chosen to take to the road, but the prospect of fresh air and a few hours away from the sickroom was irresistible. The storm she saw rising in the west would break probably in three or four hours, and she would be home well before that time.

Miss Tyson had preserved the silver rose for Mrs. Fletcher. ''I did think she would think better of her little temper, Miss Standish. I know her well, you see.''

Fenella did not wish to gossip about her employer, but took the rose, wrapped in paper, and left on her other errands. Miss Tyson had not missed the involuntary stiffening of Mrs. Fletcher's servant, repelling her attempt to establish confidences between them. She thought she was too good to coze with a seamstress, did she? Well, Miss Tyson, who was on excellent terms with the housekeeper at the vicarage, knew better.

Fenella had completed her errands and was retracing her steps to the inn, where Francis, the groom, had taken the curricle. The vicar's wife, approaching on the opposite pavement, caught sight of her and crossed the street to meet her.

''Miss Standish,'' cried Mrs. Roseacre, ''I hope you can tell me good news of Mrs. Fletcher?''

''The doctor says she is well-mended.'' Fenella smiled.

''Such a tragic occurrence, and quite without explanation, I think?''

''As far as I know, there has been no solution offered.''

"A vagrant, I suppose. I don't know what England is coming to when a lady is not safe anywhere she chooses to walk."

There seemed no suitable answer to give. But none was required, for Mrs. Roseacre continued without pause.

"I am glad I caught sight of you. I have been wanting to apologize for my husband for several days."

"Apologize? Whatever for?"

"He told me what had transpired here at the vicarage gate. You cannot believe what gossips men are. Much worse than women, I always say. He was never one to use the discretion the Lord gave him!"

Fenella must have looked bewildered, for Mrs. Roseacre jogged her memory. "The day that his lordship and you were having a comfortable coze at our gate. And Vicar needs must trot out to interrupt you, and of all things pass on to his lordship that odd rumor about him and Mrs. Fletcher! Can you credit such tactlessness?"

Since Fenella had been a witness to the vicar's bumbling, she could well credit his indiscretion. She wished above all things to hear no more from Mrs. Roseacre.

"I fear I must make my excuses, Mrs. Roseacre. The storm seems to be rising swiftly, and I fear being caught on the way."

She made to leave, but the woman caught her sleeve, dangerously unsettling a couple of parcels. "Oh, my, look what I've done!" Mrs. Roseacre exclaimed, setting the parcels to rights. "I wonder you do not have a footman to accompany you."

"Francis is waiting with the curricle at the inn. I really must leave."

Mrs. Roseacre continued as though she had not spoken. "I want you to know that his lordship set my husband straight on that head. I did wish to speak to you the other day, but there was no opportunity to be private with you."

"There was no need at all to apologize to me."

"But it is something entirely else that I wish to mention. I noticed particularly that day when we went picnicking that you and his lordship emerged from the woods together. I thought nothing of it," she said mendaciously, "but I noted very particularly that Lady Clavering was most disapproving. I do hope you have no expectations along that line, for you must know that the earl is much above your station, and I should not like to see you made miserable, as you will inevitably be."

"I do not think you need worry on my behalf, Mrs. Roseacre. Nothing but mere civility has passed between us. His lordship is certainly too well-bred to forget his station, and I am more than aware of my own."

Mrs. Roseacre looked a little less confident in the face of Fenella's response. "I hope I haven't overstepped the mark," she said slowly.

"Indeed you have," said Fenella pleasantly, and stepped out quickly toward the inn and her curricle.

Fenella gave the reins to Francis. She was nearly blind with anger, and dared not trust herself to drive safely. How dared that woman warn her against Robert? How dared she criticize Fenella's behavior? Fenella had with some difficulty restrained herself from putting the vicar's wife in her place, as she well knew how to do. But, as she had said to Mrs. Roseacre, she was more than well aware of her own station!

All the parcels save the silver rose were stowed under the seat. She held the delicate paper-wrapped flower in her lap to protect it from jostling. She longed to throw something to relieve her feelings. She hadn't felt so inclined since she was twelve. How dared the woman, how *dared* she!

Finally she was recovered sufficiently to look about her. They had left the town well behind, and ahead of them rose the heights on which Chantrey Manor, as well as Stockton Priory, was built. Above the tops of the trees clothing the slope, slate-colored storm clouds moved swiftly. She and Francis might well be drenched before they reached shelter, a conviction made doubly sure by the first flicker of lightning at the leading edge of the clouds.

20

The storm burst in fury overhead.

Even as the first roll of thunder rumbled away down the valley, the rain commenced, not as a gentle pattering on the spring leaves, but as a full-fledged and immense deluge. In a moment Fenella was drenched. The rose in her lap had no chance of surviving in its original form.

Francis allowed the rain to stream down his face without wiping it away, since both hands were fully occupied in holding the horses. She regretted allowing him to drive, but there was no help for it now.

At least they would not be concerned about other traffic on the road, save the farm cart they had passed some little distance back.

The road had in the first few moments of the downpour become a torrent of mud. The trees lining the road on either side dipped and swayed in the gusty wind. Even the ancient tree at the edge of the hill strained in torment.

The horses struggled at last to the top of the hill, and Fenella took a deep breath. She was much relieved, for now that they had reached the heights, it was a straight run for the Manor. They would be home and dry within a half-hour.

She was mistaken.

At the top of the hill, the road from Stockton Priory entered from the right. The rain drummed on horses, on curricle, on the ground, sounding almost like hoofbeats on a galloping stallion.

It *was* a galloping stallion! She glanced up the road to the

Priory, and saw dimly through the rain a light gray horse
thundering toward them. She cried out a warning, but at that
moment the storm reached its peak.

A long finger of lightning pointed to the ground, and at
the same moment there was a rattling peal of thunder. Behind
them came a rending crash, and she swiveled to see that the
old oak had finally come crashing to the ground.

As in a nightmare, Fenella watched the disaster unfold.
All seemed to move slowly, inexorably toward them, but
it could have taken only a few seconds.

The horses bolted, running wildly into the side road at the
same moment as the rider shot into the intersection. The
curricle lost a wheel and canted severely to Fenella's right.
She felt Francis sliding down the inclined seat onto her, and
she slid gently from the vehicle into the ditch at the side of
the road.

The last sight that met her eyes was the rider of the gray
reining up and looking down at the scene of the accident.
But instead of dismounting and offering help, he grinned
down at her. Dolph turned his horse and rode down the hill.

Fenella closed her eyes upon blackness.

The farm cart, carrying a tenant of Stockton Priory and
his son, plodded sturdily up the hill. The horse hitched to
the cart was a phlegmatic specimen, having weathered more
storms than Noah, and remained unimpressed by the worst
of them.

When the farmer came upon the wreck and reined up, the
animal stood stolidly while thunder crashed around him and
trees writhed in torment at either side.

The farmer was much more agitated. ''Here's a hem set-
out,'' he informed his son. ''The horses I know, they's from
the Manor. But the lady, I dunno who she is, but she's in
a fair way to drownd herself there in the ditch.''

He knelt by Fenella and moved her limbs tentatively.
''Naught too bad here, son. Do you unhitch Barney and go
up to the house. We need a mort of men here.''

The boy returned in a very short time. While he was gone,
the farmer had lifted Fenella to a higher patch of ground and

straightened her skirt. She had something unidentifiable in her hand, and from some feeling of innate decency, he crossed her arms on her chest.

It occurred to him then that the lady would not have been driving alone. But in the meantime the horses, recovered from their wild dash toward the ditch, began to plunge and rear again. He went to their heads to calm them. By chance his eye fell upon Francis, on his knees, holding his head and sobbing.

The farmer was disgusted. "Here, now," he said bracingly, "do you get off your knees and take care of your horses. Your mistress could have drownded, for all of you. Such an excuse for a man I never did see! Even a girl'd have more bottom than you!"

At that moment Lord Wolver galloped up from the Priory.

"Anson! What's amiss here?" he demanded, dismounting.

"I dunno, my lord. But here's a lady was lying in the ditch all but drowned, and you willow-wand caterwauling in the road, and—"

"A good thing you came along, Anson. Your boy is coming along with the others."

All he had learned from the boy's account of the accident was that a lady was headfirst in a ditch and her vehicle was reduced to matchsticks. His first sight of Fenella arrested his breathing. She lay, eyes closed, arms crossed on her breast, with what seemed to be a lily in her hands. Dressed for burial!

Beside her on one knee, he found a pulse beating regularly, and at his touch, she stirred. "She's coming around," he told Anson, much relieved. "The men are coming. They can do what is needful." He rose and looked closely at his tenant. "You and your boy are both wet through and had best go home. A good thing you were on the road! I'll be around to see you tomorrow, to hear just how it was."

After the farmer and his son had urged their horse to a walk, Robert took off his coat and tucked it around Fenella. "I will have you home very soon now," he said softly. She heard, but she was too weary to open her eyes.

The men were approaching. He could hear the wheels

rumbling and the voices of the tenants summoned from their homes. Suddenly Robert realized that the storm had passed far down the valley.

He walked to where Francis, now on his feet, looked at him piteously. "I could not hold the horses, my lord. The lightning was bad enough, but when the tree went down and that fool—begging your pardon, my lord—that gentleman came riding full tilt into the road, they just bolted."

Since Dolph had been in a temper all the day, and finally picked a quarrel with Lady Margaret, Robert was not surprised that he had ridden away as though fiends were after him. But it was the worst of bad luck that he had come out into the road just as Fenella was passing.

Robert frowned. How could Dolph not have seen the accident? Or, seeing it, why had he not stopped to render aid?

Robert's further speculations were cut short by the arrival of a pair of farm wagons and a half dozen men.

The curricle, it was found, was beyond immediate repair, so it was dragged to the side of the road out of the track. The horses were cut loose from the traces. Francis was to be sent home with a message that Miss Standish would be staying the night at Stockton Priory.

"With Lady Margaret," Robert said deliberately. He had not missed those long disapproving stares of Lady Clavering and the vicar's wife when he and Fenella had approached the scene of Sophy's attack.

He returned to Fenella. To his relief, her eyes were open, staring at the sky. "Are you feeling more the thing now?" he asked tenderly.

She tried to speak, moistened her lips, and tried again. "If only the sky would stop revolving!"

Amused, he said, "If I help you, do you think you can stand?"

Her stomach told her it would not be wise to disturb it, at least for a moment or two. She closed her eyes again. "I . . . I do not think so."

"Very well, you shall not be obliged to. But I do think you would be better out of the wet."

"Where is Francis? Was he hurt?"

"There is nothing wrong with your groom save for a sad want of courage. Do not trouble yourself about him."

He summoned some of his men and gave them instructions. Without quite knowing how it came about, she felt herself lifted gently onto a padded plank, placed on a wagon, and conveyed with great care to Stockton Priory.

Lady Margaret, the housekeeper, and a pair of maids met the party in the foyer. Lady Margaret said, "I have had the Yellow Room made ready, in case it was needed." She looked more closely at the victim, who was now struggling to sit up, and uttered a startled exclamation. "Fenella! Is she hurt, Robert?"

"Shaken up, I should think. No bones broken, Anson said."

While he spoke, Fenella swung her feet to the floor and stood, swaying only slightly as Robert steadied her. How would he know? Fenella thought. She did not know she had spoken aloud until Robert answered, with a chuckle, "Well, he said bones is bones and he knows horses and cows, and no bones is broke on the young lady."

She giggled. Then, once started, she feared she could not stop. Lady Margaret's lips twitched, but she said sternly, "Now, young lady, it's up to bed for you!"

Brooking no arguments, Lady Margaret took Fenella's arm, but Robert intervened and picked her up. "The Yellow Room, I believe you said?"

The housekeeper and Pringle, Lady Margaret's maid, stripped the wet clothes from Fenella and enveloped her in a gown of soft flannel. She was bustled into bed, a hot brick at her feet, down pillows beneath her head. She could almost imagine herself back at Oakhurst, cosseted and surrounded with luxury. That was her last thought before she closed her eyes and fell into a deep sleep.

When she awoke, she felt she was dreaming still. This room with its gold velvet draperies and warm brown carpet was not familiar to her. She stirred uneasily.

"You are awake, my dear? How do you feel?" Without

waiting for Fenella's answer, she added, "I shall send for some dinner for you."

"Lady Margaret! You have been sitting with me? I cannot just now think how I came here. Besides, I am not sure I want dinner."

"You will take some broth and a biscuit at least. You will feel much better then."

"I cannot think—am I really at Stockton Priory? I must be, if you are here."

"Don't fret, my dear. I'll tell you everything, but you must eat first."

The soup was the best she had ever eaten, she thought, and her hostess watched her spoon up the last bit with approval. "Ah, you do feel better! A bit of color in your cheeks now. You were the color of ashes when you were brought here."

"I've been trying to remember," said Fenella. "There was a storm, and there was someone who came along and didn't help, and that's all I remember."

The maid had left the door ajar. Robert tapped and entered. "I am glad to see you restored. Shall we send for the doctor?"

"On no account!" protested Fenella. "I shall feel completely well by morning." After a moment she asked hesitantly, "Is it morning now?"

"No, my dear child. It is still early evening. But don't think you will return to Chantrey Manor tonight! I shall not allow it," said Lady Margaret.

Thankful to have the decision made for her, Fenella smiled and lay back against the pillows. "I think I dreamed I was at Oakhurst again," she said slowly. "But I am not."

"I wish you will tell me, Fenella—you don't mind if I call you Fenella, do you? You are so like your mother, whom I knew well before her marriage."

"I don't remember her clearly anymore."

"I am sure you do not. I hesitate to say that even my late husband's features are fading in my memory. But she was a lovely creature, and you resemble her. You did have a

Season, of course. I cannot think why we did not meet then.''

"That was three years ago," Robert reminded her. He had pulled up a chair, and it was obvious that he intended to stay for some time. "You were ill that year."

"Of course. My wretched joints! But I went to Tunbridge Wells and recovered completely." Robert did not remind her that she limped obviously in damp weather, as today had been.

"Yes, but we were called home suddenly. My father never explained what urgency summoned him, but after a fortnight, it was clear." Her voice was low and sad. But Lady Margaret urged her on.

"It was the debts, you see. He could not bear to see Oakhurst sold."

"And left you to deal with what was left."

Fenella caught the irony in Lady Margaret's voice. "There was nothing left," she explained. "I left Oakhurst with the clothes I stood up in, and my father's Bible. But, in a way, it has worked out well. I support myself, but I could not earn sufficiently to afford comfortable living for him."

She glanced at Robert. Lady Margaret did not seem to know that Robert had come to Oakhurst, had, from softness of heart, offered to marry her and give her a home. Catching her eye, he shook his head slightly.

There were various rejoinders that could be made to Fenella's arguments, but none that either of the Thornes wished to make. Fenella had come to terms with her father's suicide, so it seemed, and neither wished to disturb such peace as she had attained.

"You have done very well," said Lady Margaret, closing the subject. "Would you like to hear something of your mother?"

"Oh, yes, please."

Lady Standish had been, before her marriage, a diamond of the first water in London society. An orphan, she brought to her marriage the fortune that Sir Giles had spent in his vain attempt to clear his inherited debts. There were no relatives on either side to come to Fenella's rescue.

"More and more of the old families are dying out,"
lamented Lady Margaret. "I see changes every year, and
soon England will not be what it was once."

"Before England changes out of all recognition," said
Robert, amused, "perhaps, Miss Standish, you will explain
exactly what that sodden bit of paper was that you held to
with such desperation."

Her eyes flew open. "Oh! Was there nothing in it?"

"Nothing whatever."

"I left Miss Tyson's with a silver rose for Mrs. Fletcher."

"She sent you into town in threatening weather for a *silver
rose*?"

"No, there were other things on the list as well. But the
parcels will all be ruined by the rain!"

"I think some of them were retrieved and sent to the Manor
with Francis. But I fear Mrs. Fletcher will not have her silver
rose."

"What on earth," said his mother sharply, "will she do
with a silver rose at Chantrey Manor?"

"I believe the family intends to remove to London," said
her son.

"She will need more than a silver rose in London," said
Lady Margaret darkly.

21

After a night's dreamless sleep, Fenella was ready to return to Chantrey Manor. She had sustained no severe bruises, but she limped a bit, and was aware of an overall feeling of having been jounced up and down like a ball. Her gown was mud-soiled and torn beyond repair.

Lady Margaret stood with her in the foyer, waiting for Robert to bring his curricle to the door. Fenella was dressed in a morning gown belonging to Pringle, with a handsome wool shawl of Lady Margaret's around her shoulders.

Fenella's bonnet could not be retrieved, its shape warped by rain beyond recognition, and Lady Margaret had lent her a green calash of her own.

"I know it's out of fashion, my dear, but you will not wish to return to the Manor dressed in feathers and ribbons."

"Oh, no. This is just the thing. I am grateful to you for all your care of me."

"Nonsense. I wish you could wear something of mine, but you are taller, and my skirts would not reach below your ankles."

"Totally ineligible," Fenella agreed.

With a burst, Lady Margaret exclaimed, "I dislike excessively sending you away dressed like a servant!"

"But, my dear ma'am," Fenella laughed, "I am a servant!"

Lady Margaret snorted. At that moment Robert swept up to the entrance, and Fenella bade farewell to her hostess and stepped lightly down the steps.

Quickly she was settled beside him, and they entered the long drive that led away from Stockton Priory.

She noticed with a part of her mind that no groom accompanied them. But it was only a short way to the Manor, and she had no fear that Robert would make unseemly advances to her, particularly dressed in as makeshift a fashion as she had ever known.

"Are you uneasy," Robert inquired, "about riding in another curricle so soon after you were spilled into the ditch?"

She laughed. "Old George, our coachman, who taught me to ride, also taught me that when one is thrown, one gets right back up. No, I have no fear of your driving. I should have insisted on driving yesterday, for Francis is ham-handed with the reins. But I was . . ."

She had been too angry to drive. Mrs. Roseacre's kindly meant warning and Lady Clavering's vulgar suspicions flooded back now into her mind. Subsequent events had erased that memory, but only temporarily.

"You were . . . ?" prodded Robert gently.

She veered away from what she had been about to say. "I was afraid that Francis would be equally awkward with Mrs. Fletcher's silver rose, so I thought it best to hold it myself."

"Probably it made no difference whether Francis or you were driving yesterday. The storm was excessively severe."

Fenella agreed. "The lightning was enough to start with, but when the tree was hit and crashed behind us, at the same time that . . . that the rider rode out from the side, I would have bolted myself."

She had as yet not identified the rider to Robert. But as it happened, there was no need. He already knew. "My cousin had got into a silly argument with my mother, and since he could not win in any case, he flung out of the house and rode like a demon down the drive. I should judge that he had little control over his horse or himself."

They reached the site of accident, and at Fenella's request, Robert pulled up. "I wonder what became of all the parcels?'' she asked. ''I think you told me last night, but I cannot recall.''

''All that could be found were sent home with Francis last night. I thought there was no need to burden you with explanations to Mrs. Fletcher. I confess the rose was not found.''

''But you asked me about it?''

''What I asked about,'' he corrected her, ''was that sodden piece of tissue paper. There was no rose in sight.''

Fenella surveyed the scene. She had no knowledge of what had happened after she lost consciousness. Robert filled in the details.

''The curricle was just there, where you see the debris. I was told by Anson, the farmer who found you, that he and his son had dragged it to the side of the road, where it still lies. Your footman was lying over there . . .'' Robert did not think it necessary to divulge Francis' breakdown.

''And I was in the ditch!'' she said in a tight voice. ''I could have drowned, couldn't I?''

''Well, possibly, if Anson had not come along. He got you to higher ground after he saw that you had not sustained serious injury.''

''Bones is bones!'' she recalled with a smile. ''How grateful I am to him, and to you, and to Lady Margaret! Even to Pringle, for lending me her gown.''

''I wondered where you had found that . . . most unsuitable dress.''

She ignored his remark. She could not ignore his next question.

''Did my abominable cousin cause the wreck?''

''You knew it was Mr. Thorne? As I told you, I think it was the lightning and the tree falling. It was incredibly noisy, you know.''

''But Dolph did not stop to help?''

''No.'' She remembered that malicious grin on Dolph's face as he looked down at her and recognized her. He had ridden off leaving her, as far as he knew, mortally injured. She shivered.

Robert's lips tightened. He had a score to settle with his cousin, and he would one day soon deal with him. A pension, he supposed, with the proviso that he find Ireland to his taste as a permanent residence, might be the best solution.

Fenella caught Robert's sleeve. "What is that? The rag hanging on that bush?"

Descending from the vehicle, she limped to where a whisp of sodden gray fabric was impaled on a shrubby twig. She examined it without touching it and finally recognized it.

"It's the silver rose!"

"Indeed? May I suggest it looks quite as well there as it ever would on Mrs. Fletcher."

"My lord!"

"And," continued Robert imperturbably, "I believe justice would be served by reporting it missing without trace."

She laughed and returned to the curricle. Once again in motion, she became grave. There would be a very unpleasant scene when she returned to Chantrey Manor in the company of Lord Wolver. Suddenly she was heartily weary of this situation. She was not yet broken to the yoke of governess, she knew, but that rebellion was not the whole of it.

And while she was indulging herself in a steadily lowering frame of mind, Robert slowed his horses to a stop. She looked inquiringly at him.

"Do you know I have longed these last days for an opportunity to see you alone?"

Her hands stilled in her lap. She fixed her eyes on them as though she had not seen them before. His words were promising, and the visions of the future they might well portend could not be more welcome.

"I have waited for Mrs. Fletcher to convalesce sufficiently to free you from sickroom duty, and I shall not let you escape from me this time!"

"I should not . . ." Her voice died away completely.

"You must know what I wish to say to you. Miss Standish—Fenella . . ." At that moment she remembered Lady Clavering. Setting her cap for him, the squire's wife had said, willing to be another light-skirt, for of course he would never marry a governess!

Yet, there was the slightest wedge of optimism in her, rather like the thin pale band of sunlight on the horizon after a storm, promising finer weather. With a strong effort she stifled any hope.

"Will you do me the honor," Robert was saying, "of becoming my wife?"

The words had been said, the offer made again, and she could not believe the words she heard issuing from her lips.

"I cannot," she told him.

He was still for a long time. "I am sure of my own mind," he said at last. "I did believe myself sure of yours. Am I mistaken?"

She could see his persistence would not be easily foiled. There was a strength in him that demanded honesty from her. Besides, he gave no impression of setting his horse in motion until she answered him.

"I am more grateful than I can say to you for saving my life yesterday. But I assure you it is not necessary for you to save my reputation as well."

"What is this? Sheer nonsense! Your reputation has been scrupulously safe with me. If you are speaking about last night, you cannot think that you were compromised in my house?"

"Of course not! I am not as hen-witted as that. Besides, even had your mother not been there, I should have been safe enough."

Somewhere within her a lonely voice cried: More's the pity! She recognized for a startling moment that she would even be willing to accept a *carte-blanche* if that were the best she could do.

"You know you would have been. But I can only wonder . . ." A thought visibly struck him. "Of course! We came out of the woods together! Is that it? Some one of those biddies has upset you."

She did not answer him directly. "It does not matter. You must know that I am leaving the Fletchers as soon as I can get them to London. I told Sir Eustace I would travel with them and get them settled."

"And then?" His tone was stern.

"Then I shall look for another position. Far away from here."

"Well, my girl, that will not take place. You cannot refuse me because of Lady Clavering, a woman we scarcely know. I wish you would take off that foolish bonnet and look at me."

The spring sun was warm on her head. She held Lady Margaret's bonnet in her lap. Robert took her chin in one hand and turned her face to his. He searched her expression, and at last seemed pleased with what he saw.

"Will you?" he asked simply.

With everything she ever dreamed of now hers for the taking, she took it. "Yes. Yes, Robert, I will."

After an unmeasured space of time spent in celebrating the milestone agreement just reached, they started again for Chantrey Manor. Fenella was unaware even of breathing. She knew there were things she must do, she expected a vexing scene when she arrived home, but just now all that was required of her was to drift in joyous lassitude. She had no words for this pervading happiness. But, judging from the glimpse she had of Robert's smiling face, there was no need for words.

When the silence was broken at last, it was by Fenella. "Do you know, I dread telling the Fletchers."

"Is there need to do so? Of course they must know. But will it be less trying for you to get them to London first—as you intimated a few moments ago—and then marry me quite quietly?"

"Perhaps so. Sir Eustace particularly charged me with managing the removal to Lady Crewe's in London. I shall leave the family after that."

She wondered where she would go. She would not need to seek a new position now, but she had no family to whom to repair to await her wedding day. "Besides," she said, "they have not yet decided precisely when they will travel."

"In the meantime, you will be required to remain at the Manor, subject to all kinds of insults from Mrs. Fletcher and her friends? I think not."

"Perhaps they will have decided today that they will go a fortnight hence. I must tell you that their decisions have a way of changing daily, if not from morning to afternoon."

"How could you have thought I was interested in that woman?"

"She told me so. And I did not think you could ever stoop to a governess, since you have such a heavy responsibility to your family to marry advantageously."

"I know no governess," he told her roughly. "I know a fine and beautiful lady who has been undervalued for much of her life. And most unjustly of all, by me." He turned to her. "That situation will be changed within a fortnight!"

"Oh, no, not so soon!" she protested. "They may not go at once, you know, even though Charlotte is now most anxious to go."

"I think she needs to be carefully watched, and I may drop a hint to Sir Eustace to that effect. My cousin, I know, has ambitions in that direction. Very well, my dearest, a fortnight may be too precipitate. I will allow these abominable Fletchers one month, after which I will carry you off and wed you out of hand by special license!"

This delightful prospect being entirely acceptable to Fenella, she did not lift a finger to prevent him from pulling her to him and kissing her quite thoroughly. When he released her, he said ruefully, "One month may strain my patience to the utmost. But I've waited for three years for this moment, and I suppose one more month will pass soon enough."

22

The household at Chantrey Manor greeted Fenella warmly. Sir Eustace roared, "Glad to see you back! Said you were drowning in a ditch. That rattle-brained groom, what's-his-name, will remember this piece of work the rest of his life!"

"You did not dismiss him, I hope? The storm was truly violent, and when lightning struck the great oak at the edge of the road, no one could have held the horses." Tactfully she added, "Except you, sir, of course."

In answer to their questions, she explained that she was not hurt—"save for some soreness that will not last"—but that she found herself unaccountably weary.

Sophy seemed greatly subdued, as she had been since Sir Eustace had spoken to her behind closed doors. Was that only the day before? Fenella hoped devoutly that the events of the past hour were not marked clearly on her features. At any rate, Sophy made little of the loss of the rose.

Emma, hearing that her governess had returned safely, rushed down from the schoolroom. Throwing her arms around Fenella, she exclaimed, "You're all right! I cried when I heard you were hurt."

"Where did you get that frowzy gown?" Charlotte interrupted.

"My own was sadly torn," said Fenella in an apologetic way. "I should not have wished to ride in the public way so attired. Besides, it was still wet this morning."

"And that bonnet!" Charlotte eyed it with disgust.

"It's called a calash," began Fenella.

"My mother had one," said Sophy surprisingly. "They called it a 'shy bonnet' in her day. You see how it hides the features." She glanced suspiciously at Fenella. "I suspect you borrowed that gown from one of the maids at the Priory. But no maid ever had a bonnet like this!"

"Lady Margaret insisted I borrow this one of hers. I shall send it back promptly."

At that moment, unfortunately, she remembered Robert ordering her to take it off, and she flushed. No one seemed to notice, and shortly she made her escape upstairs.

Muggins, confined to his idol's bedchamber overnight, now greeted her with delirious joy, racing around her three times before she could catch him. She picked him up and crooned to him, while the maid confessed, "I'm that glad to see you, miss, but I should tell you I dropped your Bible on the floor when I was cleaning this morning. Thought I'd give the room a good redd-out as long as you weren't home, and I dunno how it happened, but there it was on the floor."

Fenella suddenly felt as exhausted as one might expect after twenty-four hours of anger, storm, a sojourn in a very wet ditch, and a proposal of marriage.

"I'll keep Muggins here, Maggie. Don't worry about the Bible. I'm sure you did not mean to drop it."

"That's right, miss. I didn't mean it."

After she was gone, Fenella picked up the Bible from where Maggie had left it on a small table next to the chair by the hearth. This moment was the first she had been alone for days. Even in that luxurious bedroom at the Priory where she had been put after her accident, she had awakened to find Lady Margaret keeping vigil over her.

Now there was no one but Muggins.

She was not alone, though, in her thoughts. Holding her father's last, and indeed only gift to her, she conjured up his features in her memory. How much she wished she could tell Papa about the marvelous second chance that had come her way! He would have been so happy for her. Perhaps he was even now in some unclear way aware of her happiness. She hoped so.

Muggins had come to lie down at her feet, his paws on her ankle. He was clearly determined not to let her get away again. She had no intention of moving. She laid her head back and closed her eyes. She would say to Sir Giles . . .

The Bible slid from her lap and fell with a thump on the floor. She awoke with a start, her mind muddled with sleep.

"What was that sound?" she demanded of Muggins, who whined indignantly, since the book had nearly struck him.

She picked up the Bible. The covering was loose indeed, but whether it had come loose when Maggie dropped it or whether this last fall had inflicted the damage was hard to tell. No matter, for it must be repaired. She lifted the covering carefully, to see precisely what would be needed to make the book whole again.

The covering was of black leather, crumbling a bit at the edges from age. A small bit of white caught her eye. It seemed to be something tucked into a slot in the leather. Some old books did have, she knew, concealed hiding places for private documents. Perhaps her grandfather had put away some papers to keep them safe, and had forgotten them.

The item was reluctant to emerge, but she worked with her fingers to loosen it, and at last she held two small pages, tightly folded and covered with writing, in her hands.

Spreading it out on her lap, she felt a chill. She had wished so much to talk to her father, and here was a letter from him, almost as though he had heard her and promptly sent her a message.

The first line read, "My dear daughter . . ."

She was overcome. Tears stung her eyes and the writing blurred. After long moments she wiped her eyes finally and began again to read: "My dear daughter, If you are reading this, it means I am already in the cemetery."

Quickly she read the entire two pages. She missed a few words, because the handwriting was that of a man deeply agitated. The message, however, was one she could not credit. It made no sense whatever.

She had been told, and had finally resigned herself to believing it, that her father, overwhelmed by enormous debts, could not face the scandal and had shot himself with his own gun. She had not believed he was such a coward, but all the facts militated against her faith in him, and finally she conceded that she did not know him as well as she thought.

But what he was saying in this letter was equally difficult of belief.

She read it again, and a third time, very slowly:

. . . . cemetery. As you recall, the death of young Brumm has troubled me greatly. Just a lad, but with much promise, a tragedy his life snuffed out without more reason than that he was innocently in the wrong place.

The result of inquiries I have had made over these three months indicates that a certain gentleman, RT, is the boy's killer. I know who he is—member of a respected family and kin to our next neighbor. I would scarcely credit this, save that the man in question has lived roughly and with violence.

Now to my purpose: I am sailing now to a rendezvous with him, made through an intermediary. For the sake of his family, as a matter of honor, I wish to give him the opportunity to make amends to Brumm's parents befor I lodge my information with the authorities. If I do not return, you will know that RT is my murderer.

If all goes well, when I return I will remove this letter from its hiding place.

Believe me, Fenella, I have always loved you very much, and if God is willing, I always will.

Your devoted father,
Giles Standish

She sat numbly, unaware that Muggins, sensing her distress, stood up with his paws on her knee and licked her cheek. Three times there came knocks at the door, and she did not answer.

Her father had not committed suicide. He had been murdered. And while she had longed to have proof that she was right, such proof could not have come at a worse time.

RT—she knew it, positively *knew* it—was Robert Thorne.

He could be no other. And she had this very day put her life in the hands of her father's murderer.

Maybe not . . .

She read the letter again, dwelling on the words that had seemed proof to her: "RT is the boy's killer."

Robert Thorne—it could be nobody else. But what an odd way to put it. Indeed, the entire letter was stilted, not written as clearly as she would expect of her father.

"Kin to our next neighbor." Next neighbor to the Standishes was the old Earl of Wolver, and Robert was his heir!

"Lived roughly and with violence." Robert had been with the armies in the Peninsula fighting against Napoleon's army—rough and violent. There could be no mistake. It all fit too well.

Her father's final conclusion: "RT is my murderer."

She felt life draining out of her. She felt limp, insubstantial, like the tissue paper in the rain, its precious silver rose gone.

Before dark came, bringing Maggie with a supper tray, she had made her way through doubt to certainly. She could not marry Robert. She had thought she was willing to contract even a left-handed alliance, so deeply did she love him, but she could not marry her father's murderer, not ever.

She could not remain forever in her room, refusing supper, not answering knocks. The next morning she rose, dressed herself, sent Muggins up to the schoolroom, and herself descended to breakfast.

Toying with her teacup, she had not appetite for food. Her mirror had told her she was hollow-eyed and pale, but Sophy and Sir Eustace blamed her appearance on her accident.

"How fortunate," said Sophy, reaching for the marmalade for her biscuit, "that Lord Wolver was near at hand. How came he to be there?"

Fenella went over the accident, remembering that they had not had a firsthand account other than the garbled tale of Francis. Every mention of Lord Wolver, and there were many, afflicted her like a fresh stab wound. At last their curiosity abated, and she thought she could get through the day. She had not expected Lord Wolver himself to call.

She should have. Lord Wolver's manners were faultless, and it was merely civil to call to see how the injured lady fared.

When he was announced, she started. She and Sophy were in the salon, their handwork in their laps, when he entered. He thought: So like that first day's visit, when Fenella excused herself and I did not see her again for many days.

How much had happened! His Fenella would be discreet, of course, but he knew she would be pleased to see him this time.

His Fenella, however, to his enormous surprise, rose, gathered up her sewing, and stony-eyed, swept past him to the door, pulling her skirt aside as though fearing to be defiled by touching his garments.

With difficulty he refrained from gaping at her as she went by, or calling after her, so surprised was he. Instead, she left him in the clutches, so to speak, of Mrs. Fletcher. He hardly knew what he said before sufficient time had elapsed that he could take a civil departure.

Something had obviously happened, something of great moment, since he had set her, his betrothed, down at the entrance of Chantrey Manor only yesterday.

He knew she was changeable in her moods, recognizing the battle she fought between governess and lady. But such a sudden change, a truly arctic chill, was not in her character. He was not to be put off by this unaccountable behavior, for he would rather live a stormy life with her than a beautifically serene one with anyone else.

He was not put off. Her persisted. He called daily. He sent notes that were returned to him unopened. At last, on the tenth day, his obstinacy provided a small return. The butler, in a most sympathetic manner, handed him a folded note from Miss Standish: "My lord, I cannot marry you. Pray do not harass me further."

As a pattern of civility, it did not come up to the mark. It held not the slightest tinge of regret. As to the explanation he felt was due him, it was totally lacking.

The wording, too, was strange, almost as though it were written under duress. But who in this household could exercise that compelling an influence?

He would not let her go, not unless she told him with her own lips why she had turned him down. It was very clear that, since his ordinary courteous attempts to see her had failed, stern measures were required.

This time he would not tamely submit to her maidenly crotchets! he thought savagely.

He had not been on the army's general staff for nothing. He had learned much that he had not expected to carry with him when he returned to civilian life.

He began to plan his campaign even before he reached Stockton Priory.

23

Diligently Robert searched his conscience, and found it comparitively clear.

It was true that she had rejected his offer at first. However, after the rubbishy gossip of the ladies in the town had been swept aside, Fenella had accepted him without reservations.

For a moment he savored the sweetness of her body pressed against his, her lips yielding beneath his own.

Something had obviously occurred between the moment when he set her down before the entrance to Chantrey Manor and the next day, when she thoroughly snubbed him. That unkind cut had not been a fancy of his imagination, either, for she had refused to meet him and had even sent him the note that rustled in his pocket at this moment: ''Pray do not harass me . . .''

She could have chosen no words that would have hurt him more keenly. Far from harassing her, his only wish was to hold her tight against the dangers of the world, to keep her safe from want and unhappiness! Harass her, indeed!

It was likely, he thought later, that that one word stung him into action.

When he returned to the Priory, he passed his mother with a word, and closed himself in his library. He sat behind his desk, hands folded in front of him, a brooding expression on his face. Several hours later, having considered the matter from all sides, he hit upon a scheme. Fenella must tell him what had risen as an insurmountable barrier between them, and he believed he knew how to extract the information from her.

For several days he made no attempt to see her. He avoided Chantrey Manor as though its inhabitants were plague-stricken. He spent days with his farm agent, and evenings playing piquet with Lady Margaret.

And he sent for his light traveling chaise and a pair of chestnuts, designated by the knowledgeable as high-steppers.

Dolph had found it advisable to travel to London. Since his heiress was guarded too strictly for him to make rendezvous with her, and since his rich cousin apparently intended to husband his wealth and not share it, Dolph saw his last chance at repairing his own fortune to lie at the gaming tables. Robert scarcely missed him.

At length the day came when he must hazard his future.

Fenella should by now believe she had sent him away for good. He had lifted the siege of Chantrey Manor, and hoped she would be beguiled into thinking it safe to walk again in the grassy lane beyond the orchard.

He left Stockton Priory, driving the chaise himself. To his mother he said, "Do not worry if I am gone a few days."

Lady Margaret was well aware that something had gone amiss with her son's suit, and she deplored it. She liked Fenella very much, and believed that of all the ladies in the world, she would suit Robert best. She had been greatly disturbed at his expression a week before when he returned from Chantrey Manor.

However, Robert had told her recently that he could conduct his own matrimonial campaigns. She doubted the truth of his claim, but she could not, at least at this moment, interfere.

He drove by a devious route to the forest lane along which he had walked daily to meet Fenella in the orchard. During the past week he had not been idle. He knew there was a road, little better than a wagon track, leading along his own boundary to meet a little-used road leading out of the valley. He hoped his plan would succeed before he had to drive over such rutted ground.

It did not.

He waited for her in the shelter of the woods. At last, when he had almost given her up, she came slowly toward their former rendezvous. Inwardly he winced at the sight of his love. Her pallor was pronounced, and her languor spoke of sadness.

To his relief he noticed that Muggins did not accompany her. He had overlooked the dog in his scheme.

When Fenella was near enough, he stepped from the trees to meet her. Startled, she gasped, and flushed. He took her wrist in strong fingers, and the color drained from her face.

"What . . . ? Robert! Let me go! What are you about?"

"Come with me, Fenella. I do not intend to hurt you."

As reassurance, his promise lacked substance. Believing him to be a murderer twice over, she envisioned disaster. Clearly his senses were disordered, for he was pulling her with him away from the house into the woods.

She pulled back, but to no avail. She had run to keep from falling, for she was sure he would have no mercy on her. Yet, to her shame, she knew that this was the man she would love now and always. Nothing he could do to her could change that. She would even go with him on whatever terms he suggested—licit or illicit, for a year or forever. But not with her father's murderer!

He put her, not roughly but with great firmness, into his chaise, and the pair set off down the boundary road.

"Where are you taking me, Lord Wolver?" she asked, her voice trembling.

"Where do you think?"

She did not answer. She stole a glance at his expression, and did not find it comforting. Speculation ran riot through her mind. He knew his guilt had been discovered! He was taking her to some out-of-the-way place to ravish her! He was taking her to the ocean to shoot her and set her adrift, like Papa! Often, she had heard, criminals repeated themselves over and over.

He was going to overturn the carriage and kill them both.

She was no coward. She said with spirit, "No need to drive like Jehu, for no one at Chantrey cares enough to follow me, even if they know I have been kidnapped."

"I am not kidnaping you."

Not kidnaping? Murder certainly, then.

However, he let the horses slow to a steady trot. "I must thank you for mentioning our speed. We have a good distance to cover yet today."

"Distance! I do not understand." More than a little apprehensive, she asked again, "Pray, sir, where are you taking me?"

"Gretna Green. You may have noticed a case roped to the boot. If you have need of other items, I daresay we may purchase them somewhere."

She relaxed somewhat. Somewhere between here and Gretna Green she might well find an opportunity to escape.

Her hopes were dashed. "Of course," he said, "there's no need to go to Gretna Green."

Tartly she said, "You will murder me before then, I gather?"

He slowed abruptly, and pulled to the side of the road. She looked around her and thought: So this is the last sight I will see on earth—dreary fields, not even a cow in sight.

I will not be murdered in such an ugly place! she thought. She opened the door. Robert reached easily over her and shut it again. He imprisoned her wrist, and she knew she could not break his hold.

"Murder you? Now, why would that idea spring to your mind?" he wondered. "I've had the impulse to do so, I confess, many times this past fortnight, but so far I have restrained myself."

Suddenly it was borne in upon her that Robert too had suffered from her behavior toward him. She had been so wretched herself, had convinced herself that such a dark-dyed villain as he deserved no kindness and that she had needed to make a clean break with him.

"I promise you that we will go to Gretna Green and be married over the anvil, willy-nilly, unless you tell me at once what has happened between us."

"I shall never marry you, at Gretna or anyplace else."

He ignored her protest. "I cannot have been so mistaken

as to see an affection for me in your eyes, in your behavior, that was in truth not there.''

''The more fool I,'' she said simply.

He sighed in frustration. ''All right, out with it. You owe me an explanation, I think.''

''You know yourself all that is needful. You cannot think me so lost to honor that I would wed you.''

He stared at her, astounded. ''I had thought you a woman of sense, but I see I was wrong.'' Grimly he added, ''We will sit here for ten minutes. Then, unless you see fit to tell me what barrier has arisen between us, we will start again for the north.''

Seeing that he was entirely capable of carrying out his threat, and observing no sign of immediate attack, she realized she had no choice.

Besides, she wanted to tell him that his guilt was no longer hidden. She was stangely divided. She longed to accuse him of the terrible thing he had done, and knew that they would be separated forever and that she could hardly bear it. But also she thought in a confused way that she owed it to her father to confront his killer. Telling Robert that she knew what he had done, and conveying her enormous contempt for him—that would be her revenge.

There was no easy way to begin. She took a deep breath and plunged ahead. Turning to face him directly, she told him in a calm voice, ''You shot my father.''

His expression of sheer amazement shook her. He had certainly not expected to have his nefarious deed flung in his face. But could he be so surprised unless he was innocent?

When he recovered his wits, he said, ''Your father has been dead for three years, by his own hand! How is it you did not know until a few days ago that he had been murdered?''

''It is not quite like that. I am persuaded I do not need to relate the details to you.''

Tight-lipped, he said, ''Tell me.''

''You may release my wrist, my lord. I shall not run away.''

He loosed her wrist. The marks of his fingers were still

red, and she rubbed at them automatically. She no longer gazed at him, but at the memories vividly in her mind.

Carefully she explained how she had found the letter. She told him the contents, marveling at her calm as she did so. "My father himself wrote that you were his murderer," she concluded. "Why should I not accuse you?"

"I was not even in Dorset!" Robert exploded.

She ignored him. "Because he knew you, and in honor, he intended to give you a chance to explain, to make amends to the boy's family. And he was as misguided in you as I have been."

He was silent. It was not the silence of innocence, she judged, but the muteness of guilt discovererd. There was no hope of error left for her.

She rushed to break the silence. "You spoke, Lord Wolver, of my being undervalued at Chantrey Manor. How true! And it is certainly your fault, for if my father had been allowed to live, I am persuaded he would have come around and I should not have been obliged to earn my living as a governess." His lack of response nettled her. "To think that you have gulled me all this while! Unless," she added, suspicion having just occurred to her, "you thought that by marrying me you would undo the wrong I have sustained? How arrogant you are!"

He was moved. Indeed, she thought he had not heard a word she said, but he asked her calmly, "Do you have your father's letter with you?"

Sharply she pointed out, "I could have, had I known I was about to be abducted. I should certainly have brought everything of value I had to pay ransom, except that as you are well aware, I have no jewels anymore."

"Tell me the exact words your father used." His manner was extremely grave.

She thought carefully. "He had made inquiries, he said, and they—how did he say it?—'indicated that a certain gentleman, Robert Thorne, is the boy's killer.' Oh, yes, and again at the end he said, 'If I do not return, you will know that Robert Thorne is my murderer.' Those words," she added in a low voice, "I will never forget."

"I cannot believe your father would write so. 'A certain gentleman'? But he knew me!" He stopped short as a notion occurred to him. "He said in so many words, 'Robert Thorne'?"

"Well, no, but there is no doubt he meant you. Related to our nearest neighbor, from a fine family—"

"He said *'Robert Thorne?'*"

"Actually," she said slowly, concentrating, "he said 'RT.'"

Deep in thought, he did not move for some minutes. The reins lay loosely in his hand, and the high-bred chestnuts became restive. With a deep breath he came back to himself and turned the vehicle. They returned at a moderate pace, neither of them inclined to speech.

"I think it will be best if I set you down where I found you."

He did so, and as she watched after him, he drove down the forest road at a spanking pace. She turned and walked slowly back to the house.

She had not the slightest doubt that he had fired the shot that killed her father. And he must be a hardened criminal with no shame whatever, for he did not act in the least guilty, and that hurt her most of all.

24

Lord Wolver's scheme to induce Fenella to confide in him had borne fruit of a bitter variety. Instead of bridging the gap of whatever small snag he supposed had arisen between them, he was faced with a disaster of prime proportions.

He could deal with the malicious gossip of the local biddies, since his intentions were completely honorable and he need never bring his countess to Stockton Priory again. But to be accused of murder, and of Fenella's father, was beyond credence!

Although there was no truth in Sir Giles's letter, at least as far as concerned Robert Thorne, it was certain that Fenella believed it implicitly. He could deny his guilt, he could try to convince her that at the time Sir Giles died, he had been in London, but nothing he could say would erase the powerful conviction that her father's letter had wrought in her.

By the time he drove the chaise into the stableyard, he knew he had lost her forever.

His servants, who had in the last weeks learned far more about him and his habits than he suspected, looked once upon the grim features of Lord Wolver as he stepped down from the chaise and tossed the reins to a stableboy, and found tasks elsewhere commanding their immediate attention. There were those fighting in the Peninsula who would have recognized the expression in those hard eyes, but those in England were accustomed to gentler manners.

Lady Margaret, reading *The Bride of Abydos*, which had been sent from her London bookseller and forwarded to the

Priory, looked up at the sound of wheels in the driveway. Her son's demeanor as he left two hours before had given her cause for uneasiness. She knew that his courtship of Fenella Standish was traveling over rough ground; she longed to know the reason, but dared not ask him.

Her finger in her book to mark her place, she listened for his footsteps. He came into the foyer and would have passed the salon door without a word, save that he caught sight of his mother.

Trying without noticeable success to compose his features, he told her harshly, "I have returned, ma'am, earlier than I thought."

She recognized despair when she saw it. Involuntarily she said, "She wouldn't have you?"

"If that were all!"

She followed him into the library and closed the door behind them. Steeling herself against pity, for Robert would not accept that, she said, "What is it?"

He shook his head. "It is my affair."

"I think not," she said. "Not when you have been blue-deviled this entire fortnight."

"I did not think I was so transparent."

"You played piquet as though you were still in the school-room," his mother pointed out. After a moment, she continued. "I gather objections have been raised to this match. But by whom? I assure you I am entirely in favor of Fenella as a daughter-in-law."

"Thank you. But I suggest that you divest yourself of any hope on that head."

The silence lengthened. Lady Margaret sat in a chair opposite the desk. Robert picked up the poker and looked at it as though he did not know what it was.

"The fire, Robert," said his mother helpfully.

He attacked the blaze unmercifully, and Lady Margaret's spirits sank. No man tends his own fire in that manner, she thought, unless his wits are abroad.

Eventually, when he had sat down again opposite her, she said, "Are you going to tell me what has happened?"

"No."

She made as though to rise. "Then I shall simply drive over to Chantrey Manor and ask her."

He looked up sharply. "You wouldn't dare!" But he knew she would, without a qualm.

Lady Margaret, exercising her imagination, thought of one possible misunderstanding on the part of her son. "You surely cannot think she is pining still after that Lanceford man she was engaged to once? Fenella is too sensible to pine after a lackwit!"

"Ah," he said, the words bitter as quinine on the tongue, "but will she pine after a murderer?"

For one of the few times in her life, Lady Margaret found herself unable to utter a word. When she spoke at last, she said, "I think a cup of tea will do us both good."

"Or something stronger." He rang the bell and ordered tea. "And is there brandy in the cellar, or did my cousin drink it all?"

"I shall bring the brandy, my lord." The butler paused at the door. "The gentleman's taste was for port."

After refreshments were brought and the butler withdrew, Lady Margaret sipped the fortified tea, watching her son. He had avoided the tea, and after several swallows of cognac laid down in his great-uncle's time, the color came back into his face.

"Very well," said his mother, "now that you are feeling more the thing, perhaps you will tell me whom you murdered." As an afterthought she added, "And why."

Once started, the story poured from him. She had accepted him. She wished their betrothal kept secret until the Fletchers went, or decided finally not to go, to London.

"And the next day when I went to call, she snubbed me royally." After a week's seeking in vain to talk to her, he believed he knew how to force her confidence. He explained his scheme.

Kidnaping! thought Lady Margaret, shocked, but fearing to stem the spate of his narration, she kept silent.

At last he was finished. "You see, ma'am, all I can offer is denial. I was not there, and I suppose I can prove that if I must, but she will not accept my word against her father's."

"Well, of course, she knew him much longer than she has been acquainted with you," his mother pointed out. "It is only logical."

"Logic serves me not at all."

She considered the tale he had told her, and while she knew her son to be innocent, she agreed that to alter Fenella's opinion of him would take severe measures.

At last she said, "RT. What a foolish man Sir Giles was! If he used initials, why could he not use the entire name? Do you have any suspicions as to whom Sir Giles meant?"

"Of course I have suspicions. I am not the only RT closely connected with Sir Giles's near neighbor. But Dolph was in Ireland at that time, stirring up trouble of some kind, I should think."

She said thoughtfully, "Most persons outside the family do call him Rudolph, and I suspect that Sir Giles would, as well. If Dolph were indeed in Ireland that April three years ago, then I should like to have proof of that."

He forced a rueful smile. "But how shall we obtain that? I am persuaded he will not tell us the truth in any regard."

"Will you be guided by me?"

He had no choice, he knew, but he did not say that aloud. Instead he said, "Of course I will. My own schemes have not met with conspicuous success!"

"Very well. I wish you to go at first to London." There followed a clear course of action to follow, and at last Robert began to see a faint hope for him.

"But I think nothing will change her mind about me," he said. "If she can think me capable of murder, she has already taken such a dislike to me . . ."

He did not finish. But his mother, having a fairly accurate notion of the convoluted ways of a woman in love, smiled wisely and said nothing.

Three days later, Lord Wolver left his town house and made his way on foot to a house on Portland Square, where he was expected.

His host received him warmly. "So you are Margaret's

son! I have heard much good about you. Dispatches from the Peninsula, you know.''

Robert acknowledged the compliment. He had not met the legendary figure before, but the respect in which Lord Chelmscott was held was enormous. His mother had never mentioned his name, but from remarks made at the start of this interview, Robert suspected that his mother was rather better acquainted with his lordship than most others in England.

''Now, what is it that your mother wants of me? I shall consider it a privilege to be of service to her.''

''We wish to make certain that my cousin Rudolph Thorne was in Ireland three years ago.''

''Aha! So that's the way the wind blows. No need to have any regrets over giving away family secrets, my boy! The Thornes are good stock, one of the best of the old families, by any reckoning. But your father's brother married poorly, and young Dolph is more like his mother's family. Three years ago, eh?''

Robert waited quietly while Lord Chelmscott reflected. The older man went through his mental files, deviously connecting one incident with another.

''Let me see, that would be 1811. There was that little dust-up, but that was in Scotland . . . and you say Ireland?''

''So we were told.''

''That means nothing to a man like your cousin!''

''Apparently,'' said Robert, ''you are acquainted with him.''

Lord Chelmscott chuckled. ''We keep an eye on him. And others like him. Oh, yes, he is not the only specimen of his kind!''

He continued until at last 1811 was as clear in his mind as though the files themselves were laid before him on his desk. Robert suspected that Lord Chelmscott, who held a post of high responsibility but little public notice in the government, was in the habit of keeping delicate matters privately in his head.

''All right, I have it. What month?''

Robert told him, and received the information he was in search of. The remainder of the evening passed, then, in civilized conversation, and Robert departed with the conviction that had matters with Lady Margaret gone differently, Lord Chelmscott might have been his father. But then, he would not be who he was, would he?

As he took his departure, his host escorted him to the door. Taking care that the butler did not overhear, Lord Chelmscott said, "A word of warning, young Robert. Your cousin is a dangerous man. I should take care to go warily. I know a soldier is well able to handle himself, but treachery is quite another matter."

Gravely Robert thanked him. "As long as my cousin has hopes of a pension, sir, he will do nothing to disoblige me."

Robert had never before considered his cousin seriously. Dolph was the black sheep of the Thorne family, of course, and was more often than not absent from his relation. Judging from Lord Chelmscott's information, during his absences he was up to no good. Dolph's childhood escapades were of no interest even now to Robert, but the information about his activities three years before was riveting.

Fenella had every reason to abhor one member of the Thorne family, and Robert could not fault her for this. But he wished she had not taken out her revenge on him.

At least he could deal with his cousin. He had the suspicion that part of Fenella's revulsion at her betrothal to him was that she had been so misguided as to promise to marry the man who was revealed in her father's letter as his murderer. He could not imagine how it might feel to know that a killer's arms had embraced one, that a murderer's lips had fastened possessively on one's own.

The next morning Robert set out to find Dolph in London. In spite of his light answer to Lord Chelmscott, he had not taken the older man's warning frivolously. He cleaned and loaded one of Manton's masterpieces, and carried a pistol on his person as he set off in search of the murderer.

He did not find him in London. Robert was a day late in his search. Cronies of Dolph's for the most part claimed innocence of his whereabouts. At last Robert ran to earth one William Lowndes, formerly one of Dolph's intimates, and was able by the judicious bestowal of largess to elicit information that turned him cold.

"You won't find young Thorne at Crockford's!" cackled Lowndes. "Several cuts above him! He did have a bit of a good wager at Jackson's Gym—new fellow in the ring knocked down everybody who came up against him, stakes went sky-high—but after that his luck turned and he was with pockets to let in no time."

"Where is he now?"

Lowndes made as if to plead ignorance, but a glance at Robert's grim expression altered his plans. Truth to tell, he was more than a little worried about his erstwhile companion. "I think he went somewhere north. Nottinghamshire. Probably you know where?"

Robert knew where. He was not comforted by Lowndes's last words to him. "Never seen him in such a temper," he commented. "Said there was money to be had where he was going and he would get it, no matter what stood in his way." Lowndes pondered a moment. "No, that's not what he said. He said, no matter *who* stood in his way."

25

When Robert arrived at Stockton Priory, his chaise covered with dust and his cattle drenched with sweat, he found his mother anxiously awaiting him.

"I hoped you would return soon," she said in a hushed voice. "Dolph is here."

"In the house?"

"No, I think he has gone to Chantrey Manor. He has been gone above two hours." She looked closely at him. "You have discovered something, I think. Was . . . was Chelmscott of any use?"

He did not answer directly. "What did Dolph say when he returned?"

"I believe he must have lost all his money, Robert. He spoke of a repairing lease, but that would signify that he had hopes of raising funds in some way, would it not?"

"It would. And I believe I know the source he has in mind. The heiress."

Startled, Lady Margaret said, "You think he still has designs on that child? Surely her grandfather would not permit such a match!"

"As Dolph said to me once," commented Robert dryly, "better an ill-favored match than a ruined reputation. Do you know, I think I must ride at once to Chantrey. My cousin is a desperate man."

His mother read his thoughts. "I believe Fenella will take care to avoid his company. I should not think she was in danger."

As he turned to leave, Robert heard the sound of hoofbeats rapidly approaching at a gallop. When horse and rider drew near enough, Robert saw that Dolph had returned in haste, but not, if he were any judge, in the vile temper he had expected.

Lady Margaret seemed as calm as usual, but her son detected rigidity in her posture, and her knuckles were white with strain.

"Has he alarmed you?" Robert asked in a forbidding voice.

"No, he has not really done so. But twenty years ago I was in Naples, just before that tragic volcanic eruption. I may be foolish, but I have the same feeling now—that he is about to explode, with disaster to all of us."

"You may well be right. I found out . . . By the way, Lord Chelmscott sends his compliments. Do I detect a certain warmth in that quarter?"

Lady Margaret reddened. "None of your affair. What did you find out? I should like to hear before Dolph interrupts us."

Robert gave her a concise report on his interview with Lord Chelmscott. "So it seems that nothing Dolph told us was the truth. He was not in Ireland, but was smuggling goods as well as people from France. It is most likely that the boy Fenella spoke of as killed was one of his victims, for there were several lives lost at about the same time."

"But that was not when Sir Giles died?"

"No, Fenella said it was three months later when his inquiries bore fruit—and he went out to meet RT."

"Rudolph Thorne! I can scarcely credit that Dolph could be so thoroughly evil."

"You had best believe it, ma'am. Even Lord Chelmscott warned me that Dolph was dangerous. And you are manifestly uneasy."

"I am not at all uneasy," she retorted. "Now, hearing all this, I am quite frankly frightened to death!"

On the premise that an accusation delayed is a confrontation compounded, Robert sent for his cousin. Lady

Margaret had resisted her son's suggestion that she remove herself from the library so as not to be distressed by the interview.

"I shall stay. Perhaps my presence will prevent an eruption of violence."

"You fear for my life, ma'am?"

"For his."

Dolph had learned when he reached the stable that his cousin had come back from London. He had no fear that Robert had learned anything to his own disadvantage, and in fact did not care whether he had.

Dolph was wrapped up in the complexities of his own affairs at the moment. He had seen Charlotte alone for a moment in the morning room at Chantrey Manor, before Sophy came downstairs to receive him. His discussion with Charlotte had gone well. She was to make an excuse to ride into town, with an escort of course. He hoped that the nosy Miss Standish would serve as chaperon. He grinned maliciously, contemplating the scene when Charlotte would be carried off to the north again, this time with success, for he would not stop short of Scotland, and Miss Standish would be blamed, dismissed in disgrace, and perhaps even hounded across England for her failure.

True, Charlotte had not seemed enthusiastic about the scheme, but a few kisses and soft words would bring her around.

So Dolph entered the library with confidence and a sense of invulnerability. He was shortly to be disillusioned.

There followed the second-most-harrowing hour in Robert's life, the first having taken place in his traveling chaise with Fenella.

When Dolph wrote out the confession dictated to him and signed it with a defiant flourish, he stood up and snarled, "What do you intend to do with me now, dear cousin? For I warn you, no jail will ever hold me!"

"It is equally certain that you cannot be turned loose. There is no alternative save the authorities. I have already arranged for Flint and a stout man of his choosing to convey you to Nottingham, where you will be taken in charge."

Dolph's eyes flashed. He had been confident at the start that Lady Margaret, sitting calmly in a comfortable chair and seemingly paying no heed to the conversation, would protest such a draconian verdict upon him. When she did not, he pointed out, "Are you willing, dear aunt, to have the Thorne name disgraced and made a scandal of in the Old Bailey?"

"Far more willing than to see lives ruined by the hand of one not worthy of that name. Besides," she said with a grim glint of humor in her cold eyes, "I merely married into the family!"

Flint and a powerful groom named Worth were summoned, and Dolph was put into the heavy chariot, the same vehicle that had been refurbished and put into service for his ill-starred elopement with Charlotte. He turned to Robert, who stood in the stableyard to make sure the travelers left in good order. "How much can depend on only a small mischance!" he remarked. "Had you come only an hour later, we would have gotten well away, and my sins would not have caught me out!"

"Not those particular ones, perhaps," Robert agreed, "but there is no lack of others that will serve if need be."

The color drained from Dolph's face. Apparently he had not realized how wide and dangerous Robert's knowledge was.

Robert watched the carriage move at a slow trot down the drive until it was hidden from view. He turned and joined his mother in the library.

"I hope," she said with heartfelt honesty, "I never have to sustain such an interview again!"

"Nor I," he agreed, ringing for brandy. "Tomorrow I should like you to go with me to Chantrey Manor, if you will."

"You don't need me to intervene with Fenella."

"Nor do I wish it. But I think I must explain the situation to Sir Eustace. He surely does not know how narrowly his granddaughter escaped ruination. However, I think he must be made aware of her propensity for ill-judged behavior. It was only by an hour, as Dolph said only moments ago, that he was prevented from carrying her to Gretna Green.''

"I agree that we have an obligation there. I am sure that Dolph told them he was here by your request." She hesitated. "Do you think that Fenella . . . ?"

"No, I fear not," he answered the question she hardly dared to ask. "She holds me in such loathing that even Dolph's confession cannot alter her mind. She will think I wrote it myself and forged his signature."

"Surely not!"

"But you will go with me?"

"Of course."

Robert lapsed into silence. By this time the chariot would have emerged from the driveway and already have joined the road at the top of the hill, the intersection where Dolph had ridden out like a hurled lance, leaving Fenella in the ditch and her curricle wrecked. But the prisoner and his guards must be well into Shackleton by this time.

Almost like an echo of that day, Anson's voice came from the foyer. Robert, an ominous feeling of impending disaster creeping over him, sat erect to listen.

"Aye, it's bad news again. Dunno just how it happened . . . I didn't see it."

By this time Robert was in the hall.

"Not another accident!"

"Aye, your lordship. The young gentleman and the others, in the carriage. Looks like that old leather just wore out finally. The straps broke at the top of that rise—aye, just where the other wreck was—and heavy as it was, that great thing went head over applecart." Moved by the drama of his narration, Anson resorted to sweeping gestures. "Horses in a heap at the bottom, here. Flint and t'other one, *there*. Aye, they be fine, just tumbled a bit, y'might say."

"And Mr. Thorne?" asked Robert in a voice from which all emotion was removed.

Anson shook his head. "Dead, your lordship. Dead as ever was. Broke his neck, seems like."

26

If Fenella had, once in a while, considered her condition as a woman forced to earn her living to be unfair, she had kept such resentments to herself. Ordinarily possessed of a forgiving and sunny disposition, she was able to climb out of her depression, tell herself bracingly that she had done nothing to merit such a descent, and plunge into her tasks with determination.

This time, however, her black mood was extended, severe, and not at all easy to overcome.

If she had been elated by Robert's offer, which opened up a rosy-hued prospect of a future of unalloyed happiness, she had had only hours to enjoy it. The same afternoon she had found the letter.

She could wish that Maggie had been more careful and not dropped the Bible. But suppose the letter had come to light hereafter, after vows had been spoken and perhaps children had come. Then she would be doubly appalled to find herself in the hands of the man who had murdered her father. She was fortunate in that respect, but truly she could not feel any more wretched than she did now.

Even excessive attention to her schoolroom duties was of no help to her. Emma, watching her warily from the corners of her eyes, strove mightily to master elusive French verbs. Word had come that the French monster had been cornered outside of Paris, and very soon the Continent would be liberated from his heavy martial fist.

Even Muggins lost his playfulness, and curled up quietly on the hearth rug before the schoolroom hearth.

What Fenella needed, she thought, was a long, long walk in the rain, a congestion on the chest as a result, and an extended illness culminating in her demise. Only then would she be out of her misery.

The news of Dolph's accidental death scarcely moved her. Her days marched in slow time, one indistinguishable from another, until she thought at least six months must have passed. Even one month without Robert would be intolerable.

It was only a sennight, that same seven days that Lady Margaret had spent watching her son grow old, she fancied, before her eyes. Even when he returned from the Peninsula, convalescent and weary, he had looked more the thing. Even the death of his cousin, the true killer of Sir Giles, had not altered Robert's conviction that Fenella was lost to him.

It was time to take a hand.

Lady Margaret was received with cordiality and condolences at Chantrey Manor.

"Young Mr. Thorne," said Sophy sadly, "such a sorrow to see a brilliant future cut short so tragically. My daughter Charlotte is nearly prostrate with grief. You know how young ladies *feel* things."

Since the chariot that had collapsed was the same one in which Charlotte would have eloped had not Robert and Fenella prevented her, Lady Margaret thought the girl was well out of the entanglement with Dolph. As to a brilliant future, so had Dick Turpin had before he rode to York.

After the necessary civilities had been spoken, Lady Margaret came to the point. "I should like to see Miss Standish, if you please."

Sophy was startled. "Fenella? I doubt she will feel well enough to come into company."

A good sign, that! "Is she ill, then? The changeable weather is at fault, I suppose."

"Well, I do not know. She refused the doctor, and I have determined that perhaps a change of scene might be helpful."

Lady Margaret seized her opportunity. "Then I really must

see her. I have a notion of other employment that might be more healthful for her. You do not mind?''

''No,'' said Sophy, relieved. ''I would have dismissed her already, for she is of no use to me, except that Sir Eustace prevented me.''

Fenella was induced—more accurately, commanded—to descend to the small salon to meet with Lady Margaret privately. Sophy thought: How like Lady Margaret, to interfere in someone else's household! And yet, her proposal was most welcome, for Fenella in the sulks was a difficult companion. Sir Eustace had told her not to be sillier than she could help, since Fenella was employed as a governess, and not as an audience for his daughter-in-law's addlepated remarks.

In the small salon, Lady Margaret gestured Fenella to sit opposite her. The older woman was relieved to see much the same marks of wretchedness in Fenella as she had noticed in Robert.

''Have you been ill?'' Lady Margaret asked.

''N-no, ma'am, I am in excellent health.''

''Best tell the truth at all times,'' said Lady Margaret, amused, ''for you do not lie at all well.''

Fenella flushed. ''If you have come here to take Lord Wolver's part—'' she began.

''Not at all. My son can speak for himself, and I know he has done so. But it is the height of rudeness not to listen, my dear.''

''You cannot know—''

''Ah, but I do. I know the whole of it.''

Fenella was aghast. ''You do, and you still feel that I should relent toward him? That is your purpose in coming, I must suppose?''

''No, not at all. I came to show you this letter.''

''If it is from Lord Wolver, I shall not read it.''

Lady Margaret looked steadily at her. ''You will read this, for I shall not move from this chair until you do.'' She brought a folded paper from a pocket and handed it to Fenella.

Fenella was acutely aware that she was behaving very badly. Lady Margaret had no part in her unhappiness, save for bearing and rearing a murderer, and Fenella had been brought up to behave far better than current circumstances appeared.

She unfolded the paper and began to read.

Lady Margaret had watched Robert put Dolph's confession in a desk drawer and afterward lock the drawer. Lady Margaret had often picked the lock on her husband's desk, for he had been notoriously close with funds, and Robert's desk provided no obstacle to her.

"Can this be?" Fenella said in an undertone. "It cannot!"

Lady Margaret cut short Fenella's broken exclamations of disbelief and astonishment. "It can, of course, and why you could ever think my son a loose screw is beyond me."

"Oh, no, I wouldn't have," cried Fenella, close to tears, "but my father . . . You cannot know of his letter to me."

"On the contrary, I do know. Come, child, you need to cry." She held her arms wide, and Fenella was at once on her knees beside her, face buried in her lap.

A long time passed. The older woman stroked Fenella's head gently, soothingly, until the storm had passed. She pressed a handkerchief into the girl's hand, and smiled.

"You feel better, I am convinced."

"Then it was Dolph . . . ?"

Seemingly at a tangent, Lady Margaret told her, "Thorne blood is solid and respectable. Dolph took after his mother."

At the door, she paused. "Don't make a mistake, my dear, as I did once." If a certain gentleman residing in Portland Square was in her mind, she maintained her privacy. "If you have need for revenge for your loss, recollect that punishment has already been exacted."

Lady Margaret returned to Stockton Priory without incident. Robert did not ask her where she had been, thankfully, and she did not tell him. The afternoon grew late, and at last Lady Margaret deemed the time right.

"Why don't you go for a walk, Robert? I vow your long face is too doleful to bear!"

A walk? He had no wish to walk! But with consideration

for his mother, he set out. He did not intend to walk in the direction of Chantrey Manor, he believed, but he had nearly reached the orchard walk before he realized where he was.

It was about the time when Fenella usually came from the house, her day's work in the schoolroom finished. Lady Margaret had judged correctly the hour to send Robert on his way. She hoped devoutly that his feet would carry him in the way she wished him to go. She could only wait at the Priory for the outcome.

Robert approached the orchard walk with mixed emotions. He had been unbelievably happy here in the company of Fenella. And now he was unbelievably wretched. He must stir himself, go right away from Stockton Priory, go up into Leicester, where he had a hunting lodge, he believed, and on up to some lands he had inherited in Derbyshire.

He had been happy here, he thought again. Even Muggins had been part of the spell Fenella had cast over him. The small dog had accepted his presence without condition, clearly believing he meant no harm to his mistress, and had usually set at once to plaguing some helpless creature cowering in the hedgerow, as he was now.

With a start, Robert came back to the present. The dog was in fact a few feet away, uttering threatening growls and pawing the thick grass.

"Muggins!" he breathed.

The lady could not be far behind. He looked quickly, hopefully, desperately, toward the house. At a distance he discerned the figure he would recognize at sight anywhere on the face of the earth.

She was running toward him, her skirts billowing, her hair coming loose from its pins. When she reached the orchard and saw him, she hesitated. She took a slow step forward, and looked anxiously into his face. Did he still want her after all she had said to him, all the accusations she had flung at him?

His face was alight, and she knew.

She flew into his arms, and they closed tightly around her. He was saying loving things into her hair, words like "special license" and "wedding trip" to her great satisfaction.

At length she pulled away. "Don't worry," he said with a catch in his throat, "I shan't seduce you here in the orchard."

Her eyes shining with unshed tears, she murmured, "Perhaps another time?"

"You can be sure of that! Within a week, I promise you!"